Promise me

JAMI ROGERS

To all the readers out there who love a great small-town slow-burn romance!

PROMISE ME

Cover design © Hang Le byhangle.com

Editor: Julie Sturgeon, CEO Editor, ceoeditor.com

Proofreading: Owl Eyes Proof and Edits, www.owleyesproofsedits.com

Visit Jami's website: www.authorjamirogers.com

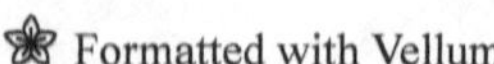 Formatted with Vellum

Love
Love
Elementary
School
Brooke's House
Ruby's House
Mile's House
Restore and Repair
Dance
Bank
Post
Collins
Luca's Shop

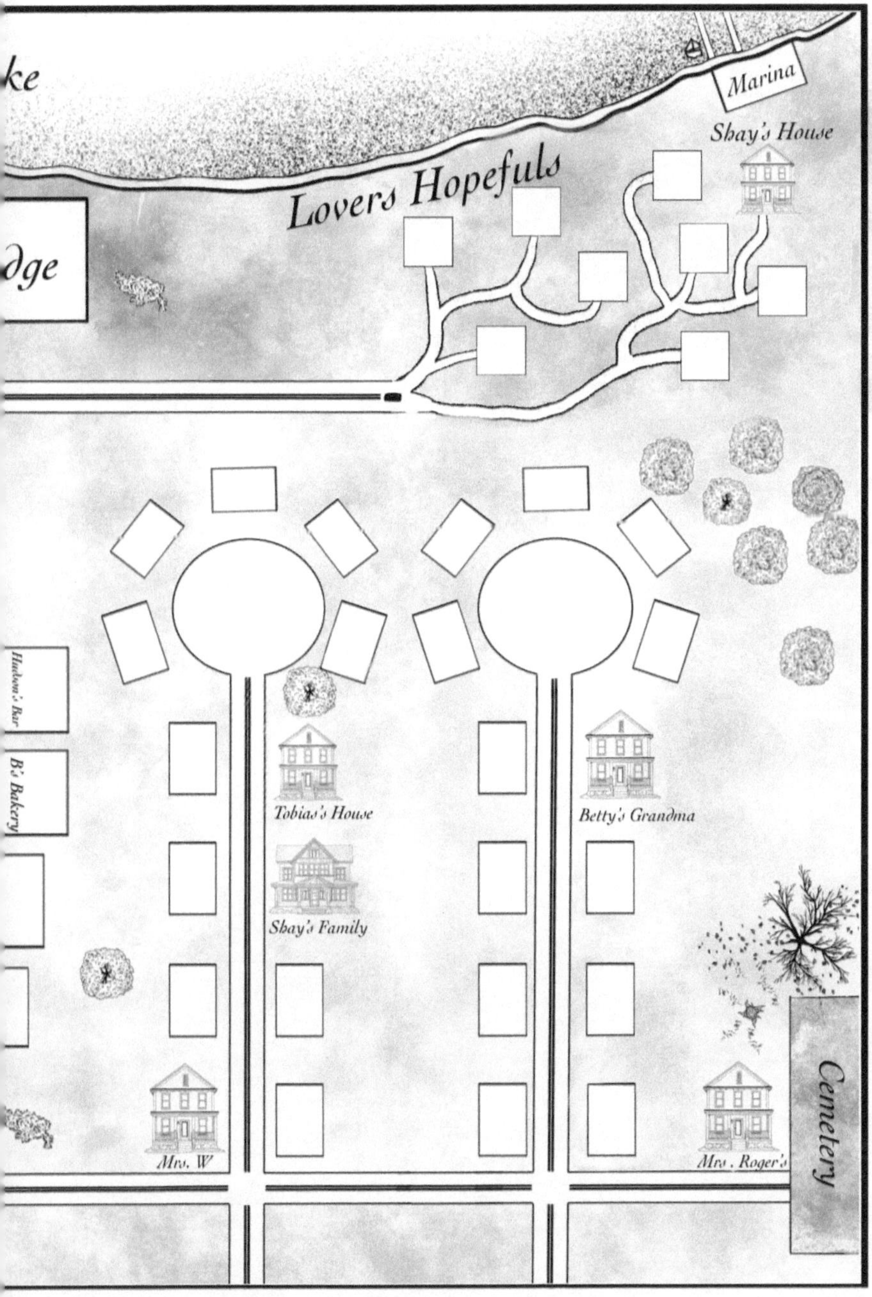

ke
dge
Marina
Lovers Hopefuls
Shay's House
Hudson's Bar
B's Bakery
Tobias's House
Shay's Family
Betty's Grandma
Mrs. W
Mrs. Roger's
Cemetery

Promise me

JAMI ROGERS

CHAPTER ONE

SADIE

"These buns look amazing."

"Thank you! I've been working hard to perfect them."

My best friend, Brooke, reaches for the silver tray I'm just pulling from the oven as if she hasn't eaten in weeks. I don't blame her. The kitchen smells like a sugary blueberry wonderland.

I yank my purple oven mitt off and swat her with it. "Don't even think about it."

"But I just told you they look so good."

She all but stomps her foot as her pleading blue eyes lock on mine.

I won't budge. Not today.

"You know good and well that Ms. Banks is coming in to get these first thing this morning."

I glance at the clock; it's five till five, meaning we are about to open for the day.

I'll be the first to admit that owning a bakery has setbacks. The biggest one is the hours, but luckily for me, I'm a morning person. Seeing as how this bakery, B's Bakery, used to be owned by Beth, also known as my mother, I was raised to get up and start working within minutes of my alarm sounding next to my ear. Obviously, at first, the snooze button was my best friend, but as I got older, it seemed easier to get up from the get-go.

"Oh, that's right. She never misses a blueberry sugar-crusted muffin order."

My Apple Watch vibrates, notifying me that it's time to unlock the doors. I hate to sound like that girl, but I can't imagine how hectic my life would be if I weren't constantly setting timers or alarms to keep on track.

In the last two hours, we've baked and decorated enough donuts, cupcakes, bagels, cookies, muffins, you name it, to get us through the first rush. Brooke will keep the ovens running while I man the cash register. At eight, my second employee, Daisy, will come in to take over. She'll take Brooke's spot, and Brooke will take mine, and I'll be done for most of the day. It's a perk of owning my own business, I guess. I won't return until this afternoon when I need to prepare dough for tomorrow morning.

Bartley, Marty, and Phil are all waiting on the bench directly outside the front window. These three are always ready on Monday, Wednesday, and Friday mornings.

"Gentlemen," I greet them with a smile as I open and hold the door open for them to walk through. "It's going to be a lovely June day."

"Great for gardening."

"And mowing the yard."

"But especially for a morning treat."

One by one, they hug me.

Hugs are a very common action among the residents of Lovers, our small town. I've lived here my entire life and wouldn't trade it for anything. Sure, it's small, and more than half of the people I went to school with had been counting down the days until they walked across the stage, tossed their caps into the air, and jumped into their cars at full speed, never looking back. But not me. I always knew I'd be a lifer.

Granted, I always thought I'd be doing something else with my life or married with at least one baby at this point, but here I am, working in the bakery my mother opened before I was born. It's the only bakery in our town, so business is good. It's especially good when Lover's Lodge, the place our town is known for, is packed with back-to-back weddings over the spring and summer months.

The town is still recovering from Memorial Day visitors, but that doesn't stop me from ensuring the locals continue their morning routine.

The three gentlemen in front of me included.

"What can I get you?" I ask, a grin touching my lips as I move behind the counter to take their orders.

Marty, with his ballcap low, smirks at me. "You ask us that question every time we come here."

"And every time we answer," Phil takes over.

"Just the usual, Miss Sadie," I finish for them in a teasing tone.

Bartley chuckles and shuffles his way to their table in the front corner. I once asked why they always chose that table, and they replied that they could view the bakery and Lovers Main Street from that exact spot. Keeping an eye on our little town and eating a good breakfast at the same time is important to them.

When I moved the tables around last spring, that table was the only one that didn't find a new home.

I plate three muffins and pour three cups of black coffee. Then I walk their food and drinks to their table, where they are already into the gossip of the day.

It blows my mind how these three have the tea on anything in town by five in the morning, but here they are, heads dipped low as they speak in hushed tones.

You know, so that all the other early-rising customers don't hear them.

"She's selling it. I thought she'd never cave and do it, but she is."

I grin, quickly returning to the kitchen to mind my business.

Gossip in a small town can spread like wildfire, so I try to avoid it as much as possible.

I pass through the swinging door and pause to look at the photo on my left.

It's of my mother and the three men out front on the day she opened all those years ago. I wasn't even a thought in her mind back then. The bakery was her baby during those years, and her love for this place never faded, not even when she took her last breath.

I hear a boom of laughter from the front of the store and smile.

Mom would love to know that those three still show up and share a decades-long friendship.

"Hey, have you read the latest book by Lena Hendrix yet?"

I step farther into the kitchen and find Brooke by the sink. Her blonde hair is pulled into a tight bun like ballet dancers, except this girl couldn't dance if her life depended on it.

I was there for our first spring fling all the way to senior prom. I witnessed the disaster of Brooke dancing.

I love the girl, but she was born without rhythm. Baking, though, she's one of the best.

"Yesss," I reply dramatically, grabbing a towel to help her dry dishes. "Why am I sucker for the grumpy sunshine trope?"

Brooke sighs, looking to the ceiling as she smiles.

"It's the slow burn for me. I love the build-up to the first kiss."

"Me too, and she writes it so beautifully. If the firemen in our town were half as sexy as the men in her books, there would be a lot fewer single women walking around this place."

"Here, here," she cheers with the measuring cup she's washing.

The bell out front rings.

When I return to the front, the smile I reserve for customers drops from my lips.

Hudson Asher is standing at the counter, his gaze roaming the menu on the back wall as if he hasn't come here four mornings a week for the last three years.

For someone who doesn't care for me and is extremely aware that I don't care for him right back, it amazes me that he hasn't found another coffee shop to pester by now. Or, you know, make coffee at home at least.

Nope. He continues to choose my place. I know the food is good here, but I have no doubt his choice to walk in here is solely to annoy me each day.

It works too.

But he doesn't need to know that.

"Let me guess, black coffee with a cinnamon twist?"

He taps his chin like he's thinking it over.

I struggle to hold back the growl I feel coming.

This man, I swear.

The only reason I tolerate him is because he's my older brother's best friend.

"Seriously, Hudson, you know you won't change your mind. You haven't in more than a year. Just say yes, and let's move on with the day."

He ignores me.

"Hudson. What do you want?"

His sapphire gaze shifts to me and darkens.

"One day, I will walk in here, and you'll greet me with *good morning, Hudson. It's so good to see you again. What can I get you on this lovely day?*"

I blink. "Doubtful."

He shakes his head and clicks his tongue.

"Black coffee and a cinnamon twist, please."

"Shocker." I fake a gasp.

He glares some more, but I do not care.

Hudson is my least favorite person on this planet. The list of reasons is long, but to sum up how it started, my freshman year of high school—the most crucial year of a girl's life, no less—he gave me the nickname of Sadie Snots. I'm not talking snotty as in *she's a brat*—no, as in the slimy, gooey, always has boogers kind of snot. What the hell, right? Everyone, and I mean *everyone,* in our school caught on to it. I didn't have my first kiss until my junior prom. I blame Hudson for that with every breath I take.

I roll my eyes as I put his order together and slide it across the counter with zero emotion. He gives me a twenty, I give him his change, he pops a couple of bucks into the tip jar, and then he walks out.

Brooke pokes her head out of the kitchen.

"God, he's gorgeous. I don't need a romance-novel fireman. I'll take Hudson Asher any day of the week."

"Gross." I gag. "You can do so much better."

"I don't know." She shrugs. "He's always kind to me when I go into his bar."

"Yeah, you're a paying customer. Of course, he's nice."

"Or"—she holds up a finger—"you've held a grudge against him for so long that you can't see his kindness."

I purse my lips. "Are you intentionally trying to make me throw up or just teasing me?"

She laughs and disappears back into the kitchen.

I spin back around just in time to help Mrs. Cutler from across the street.

Hudson and kindness do not belong in the same sentence just the same as Hudson and I do not belong in the same room for longer than sixty seconds.

Ever.

CHAPTER TWO

HUDSON

The lights buzz as I flip the switch by the employee entrance.

I sigh at the noise and make my way inside. I take a giant bite out of my donut and sip my coffee.

Three years ago, I would have balked at the idea of coffee and a donut for breakfast—especially before my morning work-out. Nope, back then, I would have walked through my oversized house and opened a fridge packed with premade meals by the highest-paid nutritionist. I would have slid open my back door to sit beside a pool I never used. Then, as soon as my trainer showed up, we would hit the gym I had turned my pool house into.

The last place I'd go to is to a bar—unless it was to celebrate a win.

Today, though, it's just after 6:00 a.m., and I'm the first one here.

To be fair, I am the one who owns said bar.

Hudson's.

I know. Original. It took me months to come up with it.

But really, I was just tired of not having a goal, of not

knowing what was next in my life. So I bought this place, moved back to Lovers, and turned it into a bar.

I step behind the bar top. There's only one opening for the bar top, which is almost a full square in the middle of the room. The liquor bottles and taps are in the middle of the bar top, making them easy to see only while we are working.

"I knew you'd be here this early," Linc, my best friend since fifth grade, says as he walks in through the back of the building.

"That door is for employees only," I remind him. My tone isn't serious, but I swear, this guy acts as if he's the one who owns this place instead of me.

"Add me to your payroll."

"As what?"

"Walking advertisement?"

I chuckle, grabbing my clipboard to note what needs to be restocked in the front before we open for lunch at eleven.

The closing crew is supposed to do this at night, but since I was one of them and my leg was flaring up, I sent them all home and told them I'd do this in the morning. Then I popped three Advil and went upstairs to my apartment to relax.

Now that it's morning and I'm tired as hell, I wish I would've sucked it up last night.

"Are you really going to work right now?" Linc asks.

"The perks of owning your own business," I say sarcastically. He should try it sometime.

Linc grabs a towel nearby and snaps it at me.

"Don't give me that look right now. Working for my dad is going just fine."

I nod, counting the seltzers in fridge one.

"Really. He loves working with me."

I nod again.

"I'm serious. He hasn't mentioned me buying him out once in the last six months. He likes the dynamic we have together."

"Or he gave up that you'd ever want to take over."

Linc shrugs. "I just don't see myself selling real estate my entire life."

"Have you told him that?"

He taps his knuckles to the bar tap and groans.

"Enough talk about me. Why didn't the closing crew do this last night? You do realize this cuts into our workout. Which, at the rate you're moving, is looking pretty nonexistent today. Is your leg bothering you again?"

"I'm fine."

Silence settles between us as I work, fully aware that he's watching me.

I know exactly what he wants to say. I can practically see how he bites his cheek to hold back his comment.

It's normal to have a flare-up.

Did you stretch it out?

How much water have you had?

You should stop working on your feet all day, every day, and relax.

Maybe you should—

"Do you want some help?" Linc asks, cutting into my thoughts.

I chuckle. "Are you still trying to get on my payroll?"

"No, I'm trying to get my workout in so I can get to work, so the sooner you finish up here, the sooner I can do that."

I laugh, grabbing the other clipboard and handing it to him.

"So eager to get to the job you *love*."

"You're one to talk. Need I remind you it's only 6:30? If anyone loves their job, it's you."

He gets to work counting bottles in fridge two, but I watch him for a moment, lost in thought.

The only job I've ever loved was taken from me in just seconds with a blade to the back of my knee.

I went from being the highest-paid hockey player in the country to the guy who moved back to his small town and opened a bar.

I'm the biggest fucking cliché there is.

And I sure hell don't love anything about that.

———

MY OFFICE officially smells like a bottle of Icy Hot exploded.

I change out of my workout clothes and into jeans and a black T-shirt before heading to the front of the bar. The lunch hour started an hour ago. My employees don't need me, but I like to be around. I grew up in this town, and even though I'm not thrilled to be back under these circumstances, I still love this place and most of the people who live here.

I hobble my way to the entrance, waving hello to my childhood neighbors and the local pharmacist sitting behind them.

The regulars love routine like it's a drug. Nothing will take it from them—not the busy tourist season and sure as hell not a packed house on the Fourth of July, where the wait is more than an hour.

I step out front of the building and find Betty, my bar manager, finishing the chalkboard sign.

"How does it look?" she asks. She stands back in army green shorts and a black shirt similar to mine and places her hands on her hips. "Too many flowers?"

I examine the sign, grinning at her impeccable artwork.

"Someone is going to see your talent one day and steal you away from me."

She snorts. "Don't worry, Hudson, I'm not leaving."

I open my mouth to say more because I'm not sure she knows how talented she is, but a flash of yellow moving across the street stops me.

Why is Linc back, and why does he have a for sale sign clutched under his arm?

"The sign looks great, Betty. I'll be right back."

Linc moves closer, his focus on the store next to me.

"No way," I whisper out loud to no one.

Did Mrs. Whittaker finally decide to sell her store?

That old woman swore she'd die in that place.

"Linc!" I call out. He glances at me and grins.

"Linc!" a much higher, yet sweeter, voice calls out at the same time.

In seconds, Linc is standing in front of the storefront that separates my bar from Sadie's bakery. That same spot also put him right between me and his little sister, who glares at me as if my presence has ruined her day.

"What's going on?" she asks.

"I'm ready to make an offer," I say at the same time.

"No. That's not how that works," Sadie scolds me and crosses her arms.

"How what works?" I snap. "It looks like Mrs. Whittaker is selling, and I want to buy it, so making an offer is exactly how *it* works."

Sadie rolls her eyes before sliding her gaze to her brother.

Linc is 100 percent pretending that neither Sadie nor I are standing next to him.

To his credit, most of the town behaves this way when she and I are near one another.

The woman hates me, and fuck all if I know why.

Growing up, I was at her house just as much as I was at my own. Her mom was a second mother to me. We had movie nights, pet funerals, broken limbs, countless birthday parties among Sadie, Linc, me, my two brothers and little sister, and more. I was even there when she learned to drive. But somewhere in all that time, she decided she was going to hate me for the rest of our lives.

Maybe it was because I dated her best friend in high school.

"I'm simply putting the sign up in the window. That's all," Linc says, unlocking the door.

Sadie and I both move to follow him, but he steps back and shoves us out.

"Neither of you are invited inside."

"You don't need to put up a sign. I'll take it," I say again, this time in a tone I hope conveys my point.

"No. I'm taking it." Sadie steps in front of me. She's facing her brother, but her petite five-foot-five form is nothing compared to my six feet. I can see over the top of her head and am staring right at her brother.

"I'm your sister," she says sweetly.

I chuckle. "The bank doesn't care about family."

She spins so quickly that her golden blonde hair whips me in the neck.

"I'm sorry we can't all have bank accounts like you, Mr. Rich Retired Hockey Player, but some of us have dreams, okay? And mine includes this storefront."

Her arm juts out to point at the empty space.

"For what? The dry-ass donuts you make or the subpar lemon bars I have to choke down with a beer?"

She gasps, stomps her foot, and then growls.

I would laugh if I didn't think she was ten seconds away from slapping me.

"I'm buying this space, so just back off," she warns me.

"Not a chance."

"Linc!" she yells, but he's gone.

I glance to where his car had been parked, but it's gone too.

Well, fuck. When did he leave?

Sadie tosses her hands up and marches back to her bakery.

I do the same but toward the bar and with a lot less fire.

As soon as I step into Hudson's, I notice all the spring tourists filling the space. We are going to be on another wait soon.

Yeah, Sadie Collins isn't going to be buying the storefront next door.

I am.

CHAPTER THREE

SADIE

Subpar.

Screw him.

I tap the plus button on the treadmill harder than it deserves.

My donuts are not dry. There is nothing dry about my baking. Not one single item.

I blow out a breath and increase the speed.

Hudson sucks.

He said those things only to get under my skin.

It's working, too, because that was yesterday, and I'm still obsessing over it.

My phone rings, and the Taylor Swift song that's streaming through my headphones turns off.

I slow my pace and grab my towel.

"Hello?" I answer in a huff.

"Oh god, are you running again?" Brooke asks, her voice calm, but I can hear the worry.

"Yes, I am."

"What happened? Let me guess, Hudson?"

"When is it not Hudson?" I reach for the spray bottle, grab a cleaning cloth, too, and return to the machine I've been using. I pull the squeeze trigger repeatedly, dowsing the screen and handles. "He's so infuriating. It's one thing to be rude in general but to talk down about my baking, about my *mother's* recipes. Gah! He's just the worst human on this planet."

I toss the cloth into the laundry bin and make my way toward the locker rooms.

Lovers has one just gym. Someone might work out at Lovers Lodge, but only if they are a guest. And thankfully, this is one place where I never bump into Hudson. Our schedules don't line up for that, so miracles do happen … even if they're small.

"He does it on purpose," Brooke says quietly into my ear. "Don't let him do that to you."

"I know he does," I snap. "And it annoys me even more that I still let it work every single time."

"I wish there was a way to get him back."

I pause in the hallway; the eucalyptus smells from the wet steam room wafting from down the hall.

How did I not think of this before?

"I might know of a way," I say quietly. Like I said, everyone in Lovers comes here. I might not run into Hudson right this very moment, but I still don't want anyone to hear me.

"What is it?"

"If I can find a way to get Mrs. Whittaker to sell to me and not him, I think he'd leave me alone."

"Or hate you forever."

"Eh, we already have that feeling for one another, so that's not really a loss for me."

I ignore the stretching my body craves after that workout, and head right for my bag.

"It sounds like you have a plan."

"Of course, I have a plan."

"Okay, well, I want you to tell me more, but the truck just got here with our delivery of necessary baking goods."

"Perfect. I'll be in later and tell you everything."

We click off the line, and I march out into the sunshine with a mega smile. I run through my mental checklist: shower, food, and then find Mrs. Whittaker to talk to her one-on-one.

I swing my leg over my bicycle, buckle my helmet, and start for my place.

Well, my dad's place. If having a headache over my business neighbor wasn't enough, I'm also a twenty-eight-year-old woman who still lives with her dad.

There isn't anything wrong with this for someone who wants that, but for me, it's complicated.

A few years ago, I planned to buy the space that is now called Hudson's. It comes with an apartment above it, and I was ready to make my move. I was ready to spread my wings and do my own thing. Multiple things happened that year to delay that dream. The biggest was when my mom died. I couldn't leave my dad all alone. Not then. Not yet.

By the time I had things together and was ready to take on this project again, the space had been sold to another buyer. It was at least a month before I found out it was Hudson.

We can just add that to the list of reasons why I don't care for him.

Sure, he didn't know how badly I wanted that place because he didn't even live here at that time, but still. He was always finding ways to piss me off. It clearly comes naturally to him.

Which is why I refuse to let him win this time. There is another apartment right above the space for sale. It's mine. He doesn't need it.

Sure, it would mean having Hudson as a neighbor, but it would finally be something that was *mine*.

I turn into my driveway, open the garage to put my bike away and head inside.

Dad isn't here. He's at work.

I let out a sad laugh.

What must he think? His youngest still lives with him, and his oldest works with him. Does he love it, or does he hate that he has no space?

How upset would he be if I told him I was ready for some of my own?

———

I MAKE it downtown in record time, which isn't a hardship considering you can get anywhere in Lovers in minutes. Still, I'm proud of the time I'm making this afternoon.

I park my bike in the back, noting how the door to the bakery is still open, with boxes everywhere.

"Brooke!" I call out. I shimmy between some stacked boxes that are taller than me and then step over another. "What's happening back here?"

"Hey!" She pokes her head out with a big smile. "So, um, I think there was a mistake on the order."

"What?"

She hands me the packing slip, and I quickly notice that the entire order is double what it should have been.

"Oh, crap."

"Yeah."

"This is fine," I say, nodding like a broken bobblehead. "I can make extra for a couple of days and give them away around town."

Brooke lets out a huff. "That's so much work, and you'll lose money. Not to mention, I'm leaving for my sister's wedding tonight and won't be here for the next week to help you."

"Swear to me right now that you will not think about work while you are gone. You are her maid of honor, and she needs you to be focused. Plus, I'm not worried about the money."

Maybe just a little.

"I'm worried about all of this going to waste," I say before she can think of another way to argue with me over this.

All we need to do is figure out where to store everything.

The fire I had to find Mrs. Whittaker fades. I can't leave Brooke alone with this mess. This will take time, and she has a flight to catch in Wind Valley tonight.

"Let's get this put away and cleaned up."

I blow out a breath. This is a minor setback, but my goal is still the same.

That place is mine.

I remove my phone from my back pocket, typing out a quick text to my brother.

SADIE

Can we set up a meeting to talk about the spot next to the bakery?

HIS REPLY IS INSTANT.

LINC

I wasn't kidding when I said I was only putting up the sign. She wants to sell it herself. Dad agreed that the company would help her in certain areas, but she wants everything else to go through her.

LINC

Her number is on the sign.

EVEN BETTER. Mrs. Whittaker loves me, so if I don't have to go through my brother, my chances just increased.

I clap my hands.

"Let's get to it. I have a storefront to buy."

————

TURNS OUT, Linc sent that same message to Hudson.

As soon as most of the boxes are put away, Brooke shoves me toward the front door. Of course, Hudson is leaning against the window of the space between us, his attention on the phone in his hand.

I take a breath before I step out the door.

Fighting with him is exhausting, but Brooke wasn't kidding yesterday. Hudson Asher is not sore on the eyes. That might be what I hate the most about him. That soft, thick brown hair on his head. The way his bright blue eyes shine like diamonds. The thick dark lashes I would kill for. The dimples that hit his cheeks when you catch a rare smile. The way his body towers over mine when he talks to me. I've seen him running through town; everything under his jeans and T-shirt is sculpted to perfection. I used to think he was conceited that way, always working out and worrying about his appearance. But the more I think about it, I know hockey played a role. Those men must stay in shape for their careers. Maybe keeping the routine keeps him connected to a dream job that was cut short.

A small part of me feels bad for what he lost.

I'm still human, after all.

"How long are you going to stand there and admire me?"

And then it speaks.

I step outside, letting the sunshine warm my skin and praying it lifts my mood and gives me the serenity I need to have a calm conversation with Satan.

"No comment, huh? That's unusual."

The sun has failed me.

"What are you doing out here? Are you giving your staff a break and letting the migraines they get from being around you fade?" I ask.

He pushes off the wall as I move toward him—well, toward the space for sale.

He pulls his sunglasses from where they are hanging on the front of his shirt and slips them on. He stuffs his phone into his front jeans pocket and then crosses his arms.

I ignore him, obviously.

Once I'm close enough, I lean toward the window to get a look inside.

She's not there. I didn't really expect her to be, but a girl can hope. I stop in front of the sign and type her phone number into my phone.

"Still think you stand a chance, huh?"

I ignore him.

I press the green button, hold the phone to my ear, and walk back to the bakery.

Her car pulls up just before I reach the door.

Even better.

Mrs. Whittaker parks and gets out. She slams the door, her hands on her hips as she rounds the hood.

"I will not do this with you two. Not today."

"Do what?" I ask innocently.

"Listen to you fight over my store." She shakes her finger at me. "Your brother warned me that the two of you both want this pace."

That traitor.

Her hands fly up. "Let's get this over with."

She unlocks the door and then waves for us to follow.

Hudson leans in close.

"She's here because I called her a half hour ago."

I roll my eyes. "Do you need a prize?"

"Maybe a thank-you since I'm letting you join us right now."

"I'm pretty sure she said I could come in, so I will not be thanking anyone but her."

"Come on, Sadie. You only want this place to piss me off."

"Oh, please. I know this will come as a surprise, but life does exist outside of Hudson Asher."

"So why do you want it?"

A throat clears, and we both snap our attention to Mrs. Whittaker, who is standing in front of us with her arms crossed.

"You each get five minutes. Now, Hudson, you can go first since you called me here. What will you do with the space if I sell it to you?"

Hudson is all business as he jumps right to the point.

"Expand the bar. Right now, the locals have to wait more than a half hour most days to eat during the tourist season, and I thought it would be nice to have a place that's just for the locals to—"

"You really expect us to believe you'll turn down a tourist if the only open tables are for the locals?"

"I would. I have this idea that—"

"You'd turn down money?"

"Sadie …" Hudson's voice is firm with warning.

With wide eyes, I hold up my hands and let him finish. Basically, he wants to create a haven for the locals. It's a stupid good idea if he plans to stick to it. All I have for motivation is that I'm ready to move out and want the apartment upstairs.

"Okay, Sadie, it's your turn," Mrs. Whittaker says.

I glance at Hudson and then nod to the door.

"No thanks. I think I'll stay. You got to hear my pitch. I want to hear yours."

"It doesn't involve you."

"It does if she sells to you and your plans become the store next to mine."

I groan and then turn all my focus to the sweet gray-haired woman in front of us.

"Before my mom died, I wanted to—"

"No. You can't use the mom angle."

I take a slow breath but don't comment.

"I wanted to open a bookstore. I always thought I would open it in the space where—"

"A bookstore?" Hudson cuts in. I know he's doing it because I did it to him, but damn, it pisses me off.

"Stop interrupting me, and let me finish."

"Like you let me finish?"

"You finished rather quickly, might I add," I say with a snort.

"Oh, you have quick finish jokes, do you, Sadie? Please, go on. If anything, I always let a woman—"

"I'll tell you what," Mrs. Whittaker says, her hand waving between us. "I'm not going to sell to either of you."

"What?"

"Why not?"

"Because the two of you have a lot of growing up to do."

"But I want this place. Badly. It's perfect for me," I plead as she heads for the door.

"Don't you want to sell to someone you know will take care of it?" Hudson's comment makes her pause, and she turns to face us.

"You're right. I do. If you two can get along, maybe even become friends, I'll sell to one of you."

I guffaw, and Hudson shakes his head.

"Once you become friends, you two will pick."

"Pick as in …"

"It would bring me much joy to sell to one of you because your parents are some of the loveliest people I know, but you two need to stop acting like children and show me how much you want it."

"By making us do the one thing you know we don't want," Hudson says.

"Become friends," I add.

"Look at that—you both understand the assignment. You have two months, or I sell to someone else. I'm in no hurry."

With that, she walks out the door.

I follow right behind her.

"Should we make a plan?" Hudson calls out.

"Does this plan include you agreeing with me that I should buy this place?"

"No."

"Then no. Lock the door behind you."

The bakery closes at 4:00 p.m. daily, so Brooke is packing up to leave when I return. I hug her goodbye and tell her I'll see her when she gets back.

I lock all the doors in the front and flip the sign to show that we are closed, and then I step into the kitchen. It's the one place I feel closest to my mom. I wish that she were here to give me advice.

Then again, if she were here, I wouldn't be working in the bakery. I would be doing my own thing.

In hopes of channeling her parental vibes right now, I pull out all the ingredients to make lemon bars. I tell myself it's because of the extra supply we got today, but really, I've let Hudson's comment get to me more than I care to admit.

I glide around the kitchen, a place I know better than my own bedroom, and have just put the first batch in the oven when my phone, which is in my purse across the room, rings. I move for it, not seeing the box on the floor behind me. The counter edge comes into view all too quickly, and then everything else goes black.

CHAPTER FOUR

HUDSON

How in the hell am I going to fix this?

No, that's not the question I need to ask myself. The question I need to ask is how I'm going to convince Sadie I'm the one who should buy that space—me, not her.

I cannot be stuck right here for the rest of my life.

I pass through the bar, heading into the back and out the employee entrance. I turn left and open another door. This one reveals the staircase that leads to my apartment and to the one above Mrs. Whittaker's store, which is currently vacant.

I couldn't care less about who ends up moving in next door. I just want the space below.

Then again, expanding my apartment could be another project that distracts me for a few more months.

My leg is a little sore once I make it to the top of the stairs, but I ignore it.

It's a reminder of how life doesn't always go the way you want it to and how you can bust your ass for years and years and still end up with nothing.

It's a reminder that I need a huge fucking distraction.

I need that space.

I'm aware that it's selfish of me to want this simply because I'm not happy with where my life currently stands. However, I also know the locals would love my idea.

Fuck.

I drop onto my couch and stretch out my leg.

Not sixty seconds later, my door is bursting open.

"I knew he was up here."

"I didn't say you were wrong. He's just a creature of habit, so I assumed he'd be in the bar."

My younger twin brothers, Luca and Miles, walk in as if they live here.

They don't.

"Please, come in," I say with heavy sarcasm.

I love my brothers, so I'm not really bothered, but a few minutes to think to myself would have been nice. Now, if it were our little sister, Ruby, barging in here, I'd be swooping her into a hug. Then, I'd be pushing her to the side to get time with my nephew, Max. He's almost six, and I wish like hell that she lived in Lovers with us, especially in moments like this one.

Miles and Luca chose to stay in Lovers from day one, and although they feel bad for me, they aren't shy about showing how much they love that I'm back.

Hence why the two of them just barge in whenever they want.

Honestly, between them, our dad, and Linc, I got pretty damn lucky with the people in my life.

Hockey was my life, and the friendships on our team ran deep, but once I was out, their life continued down that path, and mine didn't. I don't have anything in common with them anymore.

Each brother flops down on either side of me.

"What did Mrs. Whittaker say?" Luca asks.

"She said yes, duh," Miles adds. "She loves Huddy."

I roll my eyes and sigh at the nickname Ruby gave me when she was five.

"Sadie Collins wants it, too, and she showed up when I went to talk to Mrs. Whittaker."

Neither of them says a word. They both just erupt into laughter. Luca laughs so hard he slaps his knee.

"This ought to be good."

"It's not. Not even close. We fought the entire time, and now, if we want Mrs. Whittaker to sell to either of us, we have to become friends and pick who should get it."

"So, basically, neither of you will get it?"

"I didn't say that."

"What's the plan? How can we help?"

I stare at Miles. He has his own job and his own life, yet every time I've wanted to do something new since I moved home, he's been right there, ready to help.

Do they still pity me?

I shake my head and push off my legs to stand. "I don't have a plan. I guess I should go talk to Sadie."

"You can't go in guns blazing," Luca says, using his fingers as fake guns and blowing on the tips of his index fingers.

Miles laughs. "Real original."

"For those two, it hit the nail on the coffin."

Miles laughs harder.

"Okay, jokester, that's enough," I say, with a little chuckle of my own.

"What are you going to say to her?"

"I'm not sure yet."

Do I want to be friends with Sadie? Not exactly. Do I want to be able to run into her around town or join a dinner with her family and not fight with her the entire time? Yes.

How do I get that point across and not piss her off at the same time?

I've never had this problem before. People have always just taken to me naturally. I'm not overly nice or a suck-up; I'm just a normal guy with basic manners—except when it comes to Sadie.

I let out an even bigger sigh.

"Maybe take her a gift?" Miles suggests.

"A gift?"

"Yeah, a peace offering."

"Say something nice to her," Luca adds. "Do you ever give her compliments?"

I shake my head. "She'd think I was up to something."

"Well, go get a treat and give her one. It will seem natural."

Miles snaps his fingers. "Oh! Do it with the lemon bars. Compliment those. That's easy."

My face wrinkles instantly, and I cringe.

"What? Why are you making that face?" Miles asks. "What did you do?"

"I sort of told her that her lemon bars are dry, possibly used the word *subpar* somewhere in my comment, and that I have to wash them down with a beer."

"Hudson!"

"You are a real piece of work!"

My hands fly up.

"Words just come out when I'm around her. I have no control. She … she knows how to find this side of me that has no idea how to be civil."

The twins look at each other, the exact same Cheshire smile slowly taking over their lips as they turn to me.

Oh, this should be good.

"Do you like her?" Luca asks.

"Pretty sure even Dad's dog can answer that one with a big fat no."

"No, like, are you attracted to her?"

"No."

"Are you sure?"

"Positive."

I turn to grab a cold water out of my fridge. Is Sadie pretty? Yes, she's stunning. One of the most gorgeous women I've ever seen. I remember the summer when this realization first dawned on me. It was fleeting because, at about that same time, Linc started noticing that everyone noticed her. He made it very clear she was off limits, which was fine. Just because I thought she was pretty didn't mean I wanted anything more.

I went for her best friend instead.

"Okay, well, how can we get you down there to make amends?" Miles taps his chin and leans back.

"You guys don't have to hang out and help me. I can figure this one out."

Luca shakes his head. "This is Sadie."

"I know."

"I don't think you do. Look where just being the two of you has gotten you."

I toss the lid to the water at his head, but he's quick and catches it.

"That's not my fault."

"Or—hear me out—what if"— he jumps to stand—"you just make the effort of being kind for a few days. If she says something unkind, just let it go. Mrs. Whittaker is going to see you making that effort and pick you."

It's not a bad idea. Maybe she would feel bad for me and change her mind about us deciding instead of her.

"I could start by going down to buy a lemon bar and apologize."

Luca snaps his finger and points at me. "I like this idea. Get a half dozen. I want one."

"We will wait here," Miles says.

I nod and chug my water, crinkling the bottle and tossing it into the trash. I do my best to jog down the steps, a poor attempt to hype myself up.

I swing the door to the bar open and ignore everyone who calls out my name.

If I'm doing this, I'm doing it now while my brain is agreeing to be nice to Sadie.

I'm out the front door and walking toward her bakery in seconds.

Then I notice her little sign out front is gone. That's right. B's Bakery closes at four.

Sometimes, she comes in after closing, which means there is a chance I could do this without an audience.

I peek inside the window. It's dark, but there is a sliver of light coming from the door that swings into the kitchen. I bet she's back there.

How mad would she be if I walked around to the back and used the employee door?

Probably pretty pissed.

I turn to walk away when something occurs to me. I have a swinging door just like that at the bar, and it's never propped open that way. Is her door broken?

I crane my neck to get a better look.

I bet it's broken.

Maybe she should worry about her current space instead of buying a new one.

I turn to leave again, but my eye catches something else that makes me pause.

Was that?

No.

Why would there be a hand on the floor?

I back up two steps and then squat to look at what my brain told me was a hand.

What is it? Is that—holy fuck!

"Sadie!" I bang on the door. "Sadie!"

I hit it harder, but her hand doesn't move.

"Sadie!"

My fist is balled now, banging on the door so hard that it begins to rattle.

Screw this. She's going to be furious with me but fuck it.

I run to the bar, grab the chalkboard sign, and bang it against her glass door until it cracks. Then I kick the glass, barely letting it shatter fully to the ground before I jump through.

I'm at her side in three strides, my heart beating fast, the adrenaline of the moment sending me into fight mode.

"Sadie! Sadie, wake up. Come on, Sadie. Wake up. Yell at me. I just broke your front door. Yell at me, please!"

I don't want to touch her; there is blood surrounding her head. She looks so pale and innocent, and fuck!

I yank my phone out of my back pocket, calling 911 as I check her pulse.

She has one.

Thank God.

As if the current situation isn't bad enough, the smell of something burning takes over. As I answer the dispatcher's questions and listen to her instructions, I grab a towel and open the oven, waving the smoke from my face and pulling out whatever is burning. I punch some buttons, probably more than needed, because why does an oven have this many buttons right this fucking second, and turn it off.

The dispatcher assures me that help is on the way, so I sit back down on my heels at Sadie's side until they arrive. My mind racing, I look around the kitchen to see if there is anything that hints at the cause of this, but all I see are ingredients.

Flour, sugar, eggs, and … lemons.

Shit.

A pinch hits my chest harder than I expect as sirens echo through the front of the bakery.

My stomach starts to turn.

There's a very good chance I'm the reason the paramedics are placing Sadie on a stretcher.

A still, very unconscious Sadie Collins.

CHAPTER FIVE

SADIE

I hate starting my day with a headache. It hints that the entire day is going to be off-kilter.

This doesn't bode well for me, considering I'm pretty sure the beating drum inside my head right now is the worst it's ever been.

People probably won't want to be around me today. A Sadie headache means a grumpy Sadie.

I flutter my eyes open, and a beep—the kind that reminds me of afternoons in the hospital with my mother—is all I hear.

I must have fallen asleep to another *Grey's Anatomy* episode.

The smell hits me before my eyes are fully open.

I didn't fall asleep to anything. Nope. I'm in an actual hospital.

I try to adjust the way I'm lying—I hate lying on my back—but the movement to my left catches my eye.

I freeze.

What's Hudson Asher doing here?

Sleeping no less, right next to my hospital bed.

Yep.

Mine.

What the heck happened?

I clear my throat. The dryness causes me to make a rather unnatural noise, which stirs Hudson. When his gaze lands on mine, his shoulders relax, and then he moves to kneel beside me.

"Hey, you're awake."

I don't do anything except nod because, again, what is he doing here? And why is he looking at me with a sleepy smile?

"Do you need anything?" he asks, now standing and looking down at me with … sincerity.

What the *hell* is happening?

I mean, I know that I planned to make amends with him when he came back to Lovers—if he ever came back to Lovers—but I feel really lost right now.

Shouldn't he be preparing for his game this weekend?

What would he think if he knew that I enjoy watching his games? He's a really good hockey player, and watching him is fun.

"Shit, Sadie. Can you even hear me?"

I snap my attention to him.

"Yes, why wouldn't I?"

"Oh, thank fuck. I thought you couldn't hear me, so you weren't speaking."

I bring my hand to my throat. "Some water would be nice."

He's quick, grabbing a cup from the table next to him and handing it to me, holding the straw from it to my mouth like I'm a kid who doesn't know how to use it.

I let him do it, though, because, I mean, after everything he put me through growing up, damn right he should cater to me, even if I don't know why he wants to.

"How do you feel?" he asks, grabbing his phone and typing as he talks to me.

"Fine. Shouldn't you be at a game or something?"

"What?"

"Sadie!" My brother rushes into the room, takes my hand, and kisses my forehead. "Thank God you're awake. Are you okay? How do you feel?"

"I'd feel better if I knew what was going on. What could have possibly happened to bring the Hudson Asher all the way back to Lovers? Won't your supermodel girlfriend miss you if you're away for too long?"

Hudson clucks his tongue as he watches me. "So, you're absolutely fine is what you mean," he snaps.

I glance between him and my brother.

"What happened?" I'm getting a weird vibe here, and I don't like it.

"What happened was you fell and hit your head. I found you, called an ambulance, and ensured you were cared for before I left. Yet you still act like I'm the devil himself and will take any opportunity to knock me down."

"Jesus, Hud, she's in a fucking hospital bed," Linc says with a scowl. "Can you not right now?"

"That's it? I fell and hit my head," I ask, ignoring Hudson's full comment.

Years later and we pick back up right where we left off.

Yay.

I was a fool to think we could be adults and actually be friends one day.

"Yeah, Sadie, but that was two days ago," Linc adds.

"Two days ago?" I ask, this time with more panic as I try to sit up. "But Mom's funeral is this weekend. What day is it? Did I miss it?"

Linc lets go of my hand and backs up as if I just slapped him. His eyes widen as he slowly looks at Hudson, who looks as white as the sheets in this room.

"What? Did I miss it?" I ask again.

Tears prick at my eyes. I can't miss my own mother's funeral. *I can't.*

It's enough that her illness took so many moments from us for years, yet now something else is going to take the very last one I will get.

"I can't breathe," I say quickly, touching my chest. "I can't … I can't …."

Linc rushes out of the room, screaming for a doctor, while Hudson moves to grab my other hand and hold it to his chest.

"Breathe with me. In. Out. Feel my chest as it moves."

My eyes lock onto his as his words sink in.

In.

Out.

In.

Out.

Our gazes never break.

"That's it. Good. Good. In. Out."

My breathing falls back to normal just as Linc and a doctor rush into the room.

"I'm fine," I say, my eyes still on Hudson. "Thank you."

He nods, letting my hand go, and then slowly backs up to the door.

"I'll, uh, I'll give you all some space."

He turns quickly, passing through the doorway just as my dad comes in.

I hate Hudson. I know I do, but right now, I wish he'd come back.

Whatever that breathing trick was, it instantly calmed me. *He* calmed it. By the look on my dad's and brother's faces, for the first time in my life, I think I need Hudson Asher.

———

Dissociate amnesia.

That's what Dr. Hyde diagnosed me with. Apparently, there is more than one type of amnesia. He spouted off a bunch of mumbo jumbo—because holy heck, medical terminology is insane and completely overwhelming—about each of them, but in the end, memory loss is what they all have in common.

I hit my head hard enough to set myself back three years.

Three years.

Three.

To a time when I'd just lost my mom, when my plans to move out and start my own business went up in flames, and when I took over my mother's bakery.

These are all things that, according to my brother—you know, a total doctor who attended the University of Google—clearly caused stress in my life. Enough stress that my fall decided, "Hey, let's go back to before it all started."

The brain works in mysterious ways, and I hope that the sting of forgetting the last three years will go away sooner rather than later.

I curl up on my side in the hospital bed, the lights off as silent tears roll down my cheeks.

My dad showed me pictures of where I was clearly at my mom's funeral, but I don't remember it.

Did I tell her I loved her one last time? Did I make sure Dad was okay with everything that day? Or did Linc cry? He's an ugly crier. I hope I brought enough tissues for everyone.

"Hey, sis," Linc says, slowly pushing the door open. "Are you awake?"

"Yeah," I say quietly.

Instead of using the light switch, he opens one curtain a sliver to let in some daylight but not blind me.

"How are you doing?"

"Really. That's that what you go with?"

He groans and drops to the chair next to me. "I know. I'm sorry."

We sit in silence for a moment.

"So, are you dating anyone?" I ask.

He gives a small, pathetic laugh.

"That's what you pick?"

"Well,"—I toss my hands up—"I don't want to talk about myself."

The last time we did, I learned way too much. Three years of information to be exact. And all that did was leave me with questions.

I still live with Dad—okay, but I'm ready to live on my own. Or I was. I don't know what changed.

I own Mom's bakery. I hate baking, but I love that Mom loved it, so I did it with her. Why would I take over if I don't like it?

Hudson bought the space I scoped out for Sips and Stories, the name of the bookstore I wanted to open. Mimosas and a romance novel while sitting on a chair that feels like a cloud, yes, please.

Hudson also lives in the apartment above his bar, where I wanted to live.

Lovers Lodge was expanded, along with other places around town. Friends I went to school with are married with kids, and I—

I choke on my next breath and cover my eyes.

"I hate that I don't remember anything."

"I know. How can I help?"

"Stop telling me what I missed."

"Okay."

"Unless it's important."

"Got it."

More silence.

"What if it's a funny story I told you about a year ago where you laughed so hard you cried for a good thirty minutes? Would you want to hear it again?" Lincs asks. I can hear the hesitation in the question, but I also recognize that he's attempting to cheer me up.

Although, in my case, can you?

I raise one brow as I look at him. "I'll accept the story."

"Perfect." He claps and then rubs his hands together. "First, no, I'm not dating anyone, and no, I didn't date anyone worth introducing to you in the last three years."

I roll my eyes.

He smiles. "Okay, now, do you remember Mrs. Winters?"

"Oh god." I cringe. "You mean the only teacher you ever fantasized about. Yes, why?"

"Hey, keep your voice down." He chuckles nervously and then scoots his chair closer to the bed.

He proceeds to tell me about how she hired him and our dad to sell her house and how, when he went over there to take pictures, he discovered a sex dungeon complete with a swing. A swing that was currently busy holding Mr. Winters. Naked.

I might not start crying with laughter this time, but he does make me smile.

I need it because as soon as I remember again that I've forgotten about the last three years, my heart shatters once more.

CHAPTER SIX

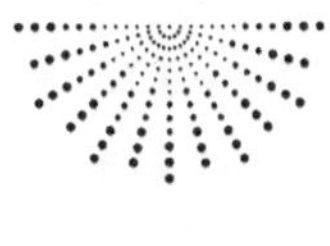

HUDSON

I wake up with a gasp in a dead sweat.

I'm not a nightmare kind of guy, but since the day Sadie woke up, I've had one every night.

It's the same thing every single time, too.

It's me waking up in a hospital bed after my knee was sliced and the doctors and therapists telling me that was the end of my career. That everything I had spent my entire life working for was gone.

Just like that.

Poof.

I never had PTSD or anything, but Sadie's face— *fuck*, I keep seeing it.

That moment. The fleeting fucking moment where you don't only feel lost, but you feel like you have no idea who you are as a person.

I sit up, swing my legs over the side of my bed, and drop my face into my hands.

Our situations are different, and I know this. Having pieces of your life taken from you—hell, I can't even begin to imagine what she's going through.

Linc texted the morning after I'd left the hospital to let me know the doctor's diagnosis.

I've spent hours researching it. How long does it last? What are the chances it's permanent? What restrictions does she have in the beginning? How can I help her?

I shake my head and head for the bathroom. I turn the shower on, waiting for the water to turn hot.

But one thing she didn't forget was our relationship. I'm the last person she'd want help from. Yet all I can think about is that she lost something, and right now, there is no guarantee she'll ever get it back.

It hurts. She's got to be hurting.

Our past aside, I can't help but feel heartbroken for her.

As soon as I'm ready for the day, I jog down the stairs and head into the bar.

I worked the closing shift last night and didn't get to sleep until about three this morning. So, by the time I walk into the main room, it's nearing time to open for lunch.

"Morning, Boss." Betty smiles from behind the bar top. She's polishing some wine glasses and wiping down our laminated menus.

"Morning." I pull up a seat.

She places the clipboard I used to take inventory last night in front of me, and I glance over it.

Summertime is good for the bar. Certain drinks and foods sell quicker than others. I mentally note which ones I might need to order extras of at the end of the week and hand the board back to her.

"We had quite a few customers asking for desserts yesterday," she says quietly and turns to put the wine glasses on their rack.

"Yeah." I scrub my hand over my face.

The one thing I've never spoken with Sadie about and thus never fought with her over is the fact that I sell some of her treats in the bar. It's almost as if our worker personas know to keep it short and talk less. It works.

For obvious reasons, there have been no pies, cookies, or cupcakes at the bar in the last few days.

Linc has kept me posted on her stay in the hospital, and I know she gets to go home today, but that by no means confirms that she's going back to work.

My best friend has also kept me up to date on the things his sister doesn't remember. I have a love-hate feel with it. I want to know, so I can't make it worse, but I don't want to know because every time he tells me something new, my heart hurts for her even more.

For Sadie Collins. A woman who has hated me for as long as I can remember.

How in the hell does her accident have this effect on me?

Is it because I found her?

Because I noticed what she was baking when it happened?

Because she's my best friend's little sister?

Someone knocks on the front door.

Linc.

I get up quickly and unlock it for him.

"The front door. That's a change."

He shrugs and steps inside.

"I was meeting the guy for the new door at the bakery."

Ah.

"Did everything go okay?"

He nods. "It's in and locked up for who knows how long."

"Knowing Sadie, she'll be back to work in no time."

Linc blows out a breath. "Considering she didn't even remember the fact that she owns the bakery or why she owns it,

I'm not as convinced as you. But I sure as hell hope you're right."

And there's one more thing to add to the list.

We make our way back to the bar top, where Betty has placed two glasses of water.

"How is she?" she asks.

"She seems fine and acts fine. She lost her memory, has a baseball-sized bruise, and gained some stitches. All in all, I think we got lucky." He groans. "I hate saying that. Nothing about it feels lucky."

I pat his back but don't say anything.

"Can I ask you something?" he asks, twisting fully to face me.

"Yeah, of course."

"She comes home today, and the doctors gave us suggestions to help her memory return. No added stress is a big one. So ...."

I nod, knowing exactly where this conversation is going. I wish he didn't feel the need to bring this up at all, but I can't imagine what he and his dad are thinking these days. I know my best friend trusts me. He's just being cautious, and coming here to talk to me gives him peace of mind.

I won't argue with him over that.

"You don't want me to fight with her," I say, finishing his sentence.

"Yeah."

"I won't."

"Even if she tries."

"I won't," I repeat.

"If she comes down here and tries to work for God knows what reason, call me, and I will come take care of it."

"Done."

He lets out his breath.

"Thank you."

I clap another hand on his shoulder and stand.

"I'll open the kitchen early and make you a burger. Eat and then get back to your family. Let me know when you're home, and I'll have someone drop off some dinner."

His head drops. "One thing off my plate for the day. I appreciate it."

"I wish I could do more."

I place his food order and let my team in the back know I'll be sending food out later. When I step back into the bar, Betty is unlocking the door, and a few people are walking in. They don't look familiar, so my guess is they are tourists.

I smile and welcome them inside.

Then I sit next to Linc again and glance at his phone screen. He's reading more about his sister's condition.

"Fuck," he groans. "There is so much online about this. I want to help her, but this stuff—I'm so in over my head. Maybe it's better if I don't do anything unless she asks."

"Being there is enough" is all I say.

He takes a screenshot, scrolls a little more, and takes another.

I watch him for a moment as a new thought crosses my mind. I've spent so much time obsessing over what I lost and how it was going to change me. I was mad that no one understood what I was going through.

But how many of my friends or family had this same reaction? *Maybe it's better if I don't do anything until he asks.*

I never asked.

How many of them spent time like Linc right now, trying to find ways to help but didn't know how to make it work?

The door to Main Street opens again, and like clockwork, Luca and Miles saunter in. They both grin when they see me, but they don't waste time rushing to Linc and making sure he's okay and asking if he, his dad, or Sadie need anything.

That's when it hits me. My people were there. I was just too selfish to see it.

I don't know how I'm going to help her yet, but if Sadie's brain works anything like mine, I'm going to make sure she doesn't make the same mistakes I did.

CHAPTER SEVEN

SADIE

I know I lost my memory, but I'm about to lose my mind.

"Here is your charger, too. Make sure your phone is always plugged in. Call or text us with whatever you need, but only use it to reach us. Keep it face down and don't use it otherwise." Linc turns to my father, who is smiling but on the verge of tears as he keeps his focus on me. "Dad, do you think we should buy her a bell instead?"

"A bell?"

He cannot be serious right now. I slap my hand down on my bed and glare at my brother.

I'm home, but it feels a lot like what I imagine jail could be like.

"Yes, a bell," Linc says calmly. I can see in the way his jaw twitches that he wanted to be a little firmer with his comment. "You aren't supposed to use electronics for a few days, and you know it."

I resist another eye roll.

"I have a feeling that using a phone for a ten-second call or text won't be that big of a deal."

Linc shakes his head. "I'll go get a bell this afternoon. I have three showings today in the Lovers Hopefuls, so it won't be till later."

Lover Hopefuls is just outside of Lovers and a little past the lodge. Technically, it's still just Lovers, but the vacationers live in that area. The ones who only stay for the summer months. The houses are larger than the standard size, and most of the families who own them live full-time in the big cities. Some are even filled with rich boys who think a summer fling should just pick up right where it left off the year before, despite the broken heart they leave you with.

I choose to curl up on my side and not reply. Linc says, "I'm going to reschedule. You should not be left alone."

"I'm here," my dad says quietly.

"Yeah, and you're a sucker for your daughter. She'll be watching movies and scrolling Instagram by the time I get back. All she'd have to do is smile at you."

Our dad chuckles and shakes his head at the same time.

"I both love my daughter and want her to get better. I'll be strict."

This time, it's me who chuckles.

Even Linc smiles.

"Hey, I was strict last year when she asked to get a dog, and I put my foot down with a no."

My laughter stops. "I wanted to get a dog?"

Two sets of golden-brown eyes fall on me, and silence fills the room.

A tear manages to escape. I don't wipe it away fast enough.

"I'm rescheduling," Lincs repeats and walks out of my bedroom.

"I'm sorry, munchkin," Dad says softly. "I didn't mean to upset you."

"It's okay. At this point, sharing a memory about something I don't remember is bound to happen."

He nods.

"I'll let you be. Call if you need anything."

He leans down and kisses the top of my head, and then moves to the door. He pauses, looking back.

"Are you okay?" I ask him.

He nods once more and then leaves the room.

"Leave it open," Linc whispers to him in the hallway as if I can't hear.

This time, I do roll my eyes.

I flop on my back and stare at the ceiling.

What am I supposed to do now?

———

"Sadie, what the hell are you doing?"

I hold up my empty water glass and then stand in front of the fridge, pressing it to the built-in filter.

Linc jumps up from where he'd been sitting at the kitchen island with his laptop.

"Dad, turn the TV off while she's down here."

Dad and I both snort.

"I'm not even looking at it."

"You might." My brother reaches for my glass. "Now get back in bed and let me do this."

"Linc, stop."

"Sadie, go back to your room."

"I'm not on bed rest, Linc."

"Just please go upstairs," he pleads.

I groan and walk out of the kitchen.

I'm halfway up the stairs when I see a picture of myself, Linc, and our dad.

I don't remember it.

It's clearly in the backyard because I see my brother's babies, also known as his tomato plants, in the background. My dress is super cute, but I still don't remember it. We took the picture to remember something. That moment, that day. What were we celebrating?

I take another step and see a picture of my mom.

My heart does this weird lurch thing. To everyone else, she's been gone for three years, but for me, she just left.

I hold back my tears until I get to my room.

Maybe Linc is right. Sitting in here is better for me.

———

THIS ONE DAY feels like it's actually been a whole month.

I reach for my phone to check the time.

I barely see that it's four in the afternoon when my door swings open.

"What do you need?"

I startle. "What the hell, Linc? Are you just standing out there watching me through the crack?"

"I was walking to the bathroom and saw you grab your phone."

"I was just looking at the time."

"No screens, Sadie."

"It was the time, Linc."

He stands over me with his hands on his hips.

My dad suddenly appears at the door with a suitcase at his side. Not just any suitcase. The stupid fancy shiny black one I got Linc for Christmas last year. Or, well, four years ago now, I guess. Mom helped me pick it out.

"Why are you using Linc's suitcase? Are you going somewhere?"

Dad shakes his head.

"I'm staying here for a couple of weeks," Linc says matter-of-factly.

"What? No."

"I just want to be here to help," he says with a softer tone.

I know he's worried about me, but this is crazy.

"I'm fine with Dad, Linc."

He looks over his shoulder at our father, who just shrugs.

"I know you are, but we both have to work, and it would be easier for us to get things done if there is always someone here with you."

"It's going to be fine. I have my phone."

Linc takes it from my hand as I wave it in front of his face.

"That you shouldn't be on. I should have bought the bell."

He takes my phone and heads for the door.

I want to yell and scream at him, tell my dad to back me up here, but I don't.

I don't know how we navigate this any more than they do. I don't think Linc is going about it as he should, but fighting with him adds more stress for all of us. He thinks I wasn't listening to the doctor, but I was. Stress helped get me here; adding more is off the table.

Even so, if Linc keeps this up, I know I won't be able to handle it.

I'm not sure how I'm going to take care of my overprotective brother, but I'm sure it'll come to me.

And it does.

I've made my plan by the time dinner arrives the next day, served to me in my room for fear I might look at the TV again.

CHAPTER EIGHT

HUDSON

"A good old time," I say into my empty living room as another letter flips around on my TV screen.

I shake my head as the man spins the wheel again.

He's only missing the "O" and has plenty of money to buy a vowel, yet he just went and landed on bankruptcy.

Figures.

I eat a bite of the spaghetti I made for dinner and lean back on my couch. Then someone knocks on my door.

I don't bother grabbing a shirt because there are only four people it could be; Linc, Luca, Miles, or my dad.

Since it's unannounced and Linc is busy, I'm guessing one of my brothers is bored.

It's weird they are knocking, though.

I swing the door open and almost stumble back at the caramel eyes staring back at me.

"Hi," Sadie says and lets out a breath.

I just gape at her as if she's some thug who walked up to my door holding a knife and demanded I give her all my prized possessions.

What the hell is she doing here?

I adjust my stance, widening my legs and crossing my arms.

She smirks.

She fucking smirks.

Sadie Collins does not smirk. Ever.

"Can I come in?" she asks.

"Why?"

She doesn't answer right away, but she, too, crosses her arms.

"Your warm welcome only reassures me that this is exactly where I need to be."

I think over my words carefully. I'm pretty sure assuming she hit her head much harder than we all imagined isn't right. But how else do we explain that she thinks coming to my place is where she needs to be?

I should call Linc.

"By all means, please take your time to decide."

She leans against my doorframe, and my gaze slowly drinks her in.

Her hair is pulled into a messy bun on her head. She isn't wearing any makeup. Her loose T-shirt and cotton shorts hit her midthigh, and her green slip-on sneakers cover her feet. She doesn't have a purse or anything else in her hands.

And she's scowling.

"Come on, Hudson, let me in."

Rejection is on the tip of my tongue, but I promised her brother I wouldn't fight with her, so instead of telling her no, I step back to give her space.

Her shoulders drop.

"Thank you," she says and walks past me, a flowery scent floating trailing behind her. I breathe deep, my heart pounding inside my chest.

What the fuck is that?

I shut the door, watching her move to the couch. Slowly, so as not to draw attention to the rabid animal in my apartment, I move toward my kitchen, where my phone sits.

"Let me guess, you're going to text my brother."

I freeze.

He did tell me to, but that's not why I'm doing it.

"We both know he'll freak out the moment he notices you aren't in your house."

"How do you know he didn't tell me to leave?"

I let out a huff of laughter. "Yeah, okay. Linc Collins told his little sister, who hates me, to go to my apartment. That makes total sense."

She rolls her eyes at me and then lies down on my couch, pulling the white fleece blanket my sister got me for my birthday last year off the back of the sofa and over her body, curling up like she plans to stay.

"I don't care what you say to him, but ..."

I hold my phone in my hands, my thumb hovering over what I should text him as I wait for her to finish her sentence.

"I need space, and I came here because you're the one person I know isn't going to baby me or try to remind me of anything."

I swallow, the pain in her voice hitting my chest harder than I anticipated.

I'll never forget the questions after my injury. It was like everyone expected me to have a plan from the moment I was released from the hospital. Are you staying in Washington? Are you going to find a way to stay with the team? Do you think you'll get a new job?

I didn't have a single answer; I only wanted some space to figure it out.

I type out a quick message.

HUDSON

Sadie just showed up at my door. I know you're going to be pissed, but she's fine. She's resting on the couch. Just let her stay here for a bit.

LINC

What the hell?

THREE DOTS APPEAR.

LINC

Yeah, she's not in her room.

I SHAKE MY HEAD.

HUDSON:

Obviously.

LINC:

I'll come get her.

HUDSON:

Don't.

I SEND the one-word text in a rush.

HUDSON

She's fine. I know our history, but I promise you, she's fine.

LINC

She needs to rest, drink water, and be in her room. For the love of God, tell me she isn't watching Wheel of Fortune right now.

I CLEAR MY THROAT, move to grab the remote, and turn my TV off.

HUDSON

She's not.

"Now I know for sure you texted my brother."

I ignore her and go back to the kitchen as if that gives us enough space from the other.

LINC

I don't like this.

HUDSON

I'll text you if I think you need to come get her.

LINC

Don't fight with her.

LINC

Get her some water.

LINC

I don't think she's eaten.

LINC

No screens, either.

THE LITTLE DOTS APPEAR AGAIN, and I grumble what I think is a quiet *fuck*, but Sadie laughs.

"You get why I left now, don't you?"

I set my phone down, ignoring the fact it just keeps beeping with notices of new messages.

"He's just worried."

"I'm still an adult, though."

I nod. "Yeah. You are."

The silence between us thickens. I'm about to head into my room when I hear what sounds like sniffling.

Like before, I freeze.

I've been exposed to all the versions of this woman, but the side of her that cries is the one I'm unfamiliar with.

I force the lump in my throat down and tread slowly to the living room.

She quickly swipes at her tears.

"Don't tell Linc," she says quietly.

"I won't, but to be fully transparent, I need you to stop doing that." I point at her, and she peers up at me.

"Stop what?"

"Crying. It makes me uncomfortable."

Her eyes have taken on a bright gold tone now as she wipes another teardrop, never taking her gaze off me.

Then she laughs.

Full-on belly laughs.

I step back.

"Coming here was exactly what I needed, thank you."

I look everywhere but at her. I'm not heartless or someone who doesn't understand emotion but fuck all right now if I'm lost on what to say or do next.

"Okay" is all I come up with.

"I'm sleeping right here too. No arguing."

I nod.

As I said, I know our history, but I'm not a dick.

"I'll change my sheets, and you can sleep in my room. Give me five minutes."

"I'm not taking your bed."

"You're taking my bed, or I call your brother."

Her left brow peaks.

"You just went right for it, huh, no pity?"

"None."

A smile touches her lips, just like earlier, so I walk away.

I typically always know what to do and say to Sadie. We have our own thing, our own version of a relationship, but smiling at each other has never been a part of it.

Which is why I wait to let myself smirk where she can't see it.

CHAPTER NINE

SADIE

The clock next to Hudson's bed reads four in the morning.

4:00 a.m.

Who the hell wakes up this early? Oh, that's right. Me. I do.

I sigh and roll over, inhaling the wintergreen scent of his bedroom.

Oh, it smells so good in here.

Is it totally weird that I'm lying in Hudson's bed?

Why yes, yes, it is.

Do I still prefer being here over being at home?

Why yes, yes, I do.

Last night, after Hudson changed the sheets and told me the bed was ready when I wanted it, we sat in his living room together in complete silence since I wasn't ready for bed yet. I got up a few times, looking at the pictures and knickknacks on his shelves. I opened the cabinets in his kitchen until I found a plate and made my own serving of spaghetti. I even grabbed a bag of baked chips from his snack drawer and ate half the bag while reading one of the thriller books from his mini bookshelf.

And guess what? Aside from a curious look here and there as he watched me, he said not one word to me.

It was the perfect night.

The only part that would have made the night better would have been if he hadn't put a shirt on when he was changing the sheets.

I haven't seen Hudson shirtless since we were teenagers, and even though it's a given at this point, holy hell, is he all man now.

All rippled abs and solid muscle.

The way his gym shorts hung loose on his hips is forever posted to my brain.

It's clear we still hate each other, but wow, he sure is nice to look at.

Quietly, I get out of bed, slip on my shoes, and open his bedroom door.

I spot his feet hanging over the edge of the couch. A small piece of me feels bad because he clearly can't be sleeping well on that thing, but it was his choice.

I tiptoe into the kitchen and open the fridge. The light comes out brightly, so I press my body against it as a shield and glance over my shoulder.

He hasn't moved.

I reach in and grab a bottle of water, slowly closing the door. Then I grab a protein bar from the snack drawer I found last night and continue to sneak to the door. I click the lock, look over my shoulder again, and when it's clear that he still hasn't stirred, I exit his apartment and retreat down the stairs.

I step out into the early morning, the air already warm as I move to the bakery's back door. I take my chances on the code for the digital pad.

2019

The pad light turns green, and the door unlocks.

So, I never changed the passcode after my mom died. Got it.

I step into the back and instantly feel a rush of emotions.

It's her bakery, but it's different. There are different pictures and signs. The shelf where she kept her ingredients is on the opposite side. The swinging door is white versus her dark oak one, and it has a diamond window to look into the front of the bakery. I slowly make my way to it but stop to look at the counters. It's so clean in here. Mom would have had flour and who knows what else strung all over the place by this time of the morning.

I'm still staring at the empty counters when someone clears their throat behind me.

My arms flail as I spin around.

"Jesus, Hudson. What are you doing?"

"What are *you* doing?" he repeats.

"I'm …" Whatever I was going to say just disappears. I toss my hands up and shake my head. "I don't know."

He nods a slow nod and then leans his hip onto the desk by the back door.

I assume he's going to say something, but he doesn't.

"I can be down here alone," I snap.

Another nod. "True, but that doesn't mean you should have to be."

I narrow my gaze at him.

"I might cry again," I say to scare him away.

"Yeah, I thought as much."

"Isn't that your cue to leave?"

"Not today. I had an entire night to think it over."

"Think what over?"

"You."

I cross my arms. "You spent the night thinking of me." My hand hits my heart. "You shouldn't have."

Suddenly, my hand placement reminds me of how he helped me in the hospital.

"I'm sorry I woke you up," I say in an attempt to tone down my sarcasm.

"Oddly enough, I didn't sleep much. It turns out that couch isn't good for anything except watching TV."

"Sorry about that, too."

His gaze connects with mine, and silence falls over us. His eyes darken to a deep blue as they study me, but it's his bedhead that makes me smile. I sort of like this sleepy Hudson look.

Normally, as a kid, I would fill this time with something snarky, but it's been three years. Is that still us?

"Do we still bicker?" I turn to the front of the bakery. I made it this far; I may as well rip the Band-Aid on this entire place.

"Yes," he answers, following behind me.

"Do people still avoid us for it?"

"Yes." He chuckles.

"What would I say to you right now about following me?"

"You'd tell me fuck off."

I grin, even though he can't see it.

"Good. Would you listen?"

"Yeah, but I'd probably have some rude comment in reply, though."

I stop suddenly in the middle of the room and take it in.

Nothing is the same as what my mother had, except for the table in the corner.

I've painted the walls and bought new shelves, tables, counters, and more.

A lump forms in my throat, and I swear it moves to my heart, stopping everything.

I gasp, my hand lifting to cover my mouth.

I erased her.

The tears hit me instantly, and just as my knees give out,

Hudson's arms wrap around me, catching my fall. He holds me to him as we settle on the floor.

His hand cups the back of my head as each breath rakes through me.

"Shhh," he says. "Deep breaths, remember."

"She's gone," I say, my hand now clutching his shirt. "And I didn't leave anything in here to remember her."

"Yes, you did," he says quickly. "Look at the wallpaper behind the new shelves."

I'm still crying, but I look where he tells me.

"I was pissed at Linc for asking. Naturally, you were more than I was, but I helped put it in there anyway. It's on the bottom of the checkout counter, too, see."

He's telling the truth. Mom's wallpaper is there.

My tears slow down.

"And the front doorframe." I follow where he points. "You left that in that dark oak trim she loved so much."

"She would hate that I did that," I say with a laugh.

"Yeah, you said that when you did it, too."

Our eyes connect then, and something unfamiliar passes through us.

Peace, maybe?

An unspoken agreement of some kind.

"It's a lot right now, I get it, but maybe on another day, you'll come back here and see all the spots where you left your mom. You honored her really nicely, Sadie. She'd be so proud of you."

The air around us buzzes then as silence fills the room.

A few minutes pass as I pull myself together. I whisper, "I wish I could remember her funeral."

"Yeah, I know you do."

"Were you there?"

I look up into his eyes just as he shakes his head.

"I wasn't. I hadn't been released from the hospital yet."

He was in the hospital?

"Why? What happened to you?"

With my tears now controlled, he moves away from me and stands. I do the same so as not to be weird and sit on the floor while he talks.

He scratches the back of his neck as he takes a breath.

Clearly, whatever it is, it's hard for him to talk about. I have no doubt it'll answer all my questions on why he's back in Lovers, but I also get not wanting to talk about yourself—more than he knows.

I wave my hand in the air.

"You don't have to tell me. I know we don't have that kind of relationship, and you probably already told me anyway, so it's no fun for you to have this conversation twice."

"Actually," he says, "you never asked about it. I assumed Linc told you at some point, but this conversation between us has never happened."

I wrinkle my nose. "We really still don't like each other?"

He just shrugs.

"Since I have nothing to lose—or nothing *more* to lose—I'll admit that I've always told myself that if you ever came back, I'd make amends."

"Seriously?" he says as if he doesn't believe me.

"Yep. Clearly, I changed my mind."

"Clearly." He chuckles.

I smile at the sound. I think I could enjoy being friends with Hudson Asher.

"So, are you going to tell me what happened?" I ask again.

His mouth opens, but he closes it and points at the coffee machine instead.

"Let's make a cup first. The sun is barely out, you know."

"Okay," I say, and I watch as he takes over.

Mom would have loved to see this.

Me and Hudson, mingling like normal humans.

He makes two cups, handing me one that is more creamer with coffee than coffee with creamer.

"How do you know how I like my coffee?" I ask as we sit at a table by the front window.

"Took a guess from when I'd spend weekends at your house in high school. Your dad would always be mad that the creamer was gone. You'd run and hide."

I laugh and take a sip. I almost spit it out.

"Oh god, that's sweet."

"Too much?" he asks.

"Let me try yours," I say, grabbing his mug before he can reply. I sip and then sigh with a happiness I can't describe. "I think my taste buds have changed."

Hudson doesn't say anything. He just stares at his cup.

I pass it back without a word. "So, tell me the story while I get myself a new cup."

Oddly enough, when I reach for a new mug and the coffee to scoop out, I know exactly where it is. Is that muscle memory?

"It's a short story, really. Two days before your mom's funeral, I was in a game. The blade from someone on the opposing team's skate hit the back of my left knee in just the right spot where my gear couldn't stop it."

"Fuck," I say, slamming my cup down and wincing. "Ouch."

His lips twitch into a brief smile. My reaction must take Hudson by surprise.

"Yeah, ouch."

"How long were you in the hospital?" I ask, my new cup hot and ready as I rejoin him at the table.

"It was long enough for them to tell me that would be my last game as a professional hockey player."

Another gasp hits me.

"But … hockey was your dream, and you were so freaking good at it."

He smiles. "You watched me play?"

"How could I not? You were mesmerizing out there."

Oh god, he was never supposed to know that. I sit up taller.

I'm about to say something to steer the conversation away because the way he's smiling at me makes me feel funny, but someone hits the window outside.

We both jump and look at my brother. His brows are furrowed, and his hands are on his hips.

"What the hell?" Linc shouts loud enough for us to hear through the window. He points at the door.

I open it for him and calmly return to my seat.

I can feel the fumes radiating from my brother. It's probably because he's up so damn early for who knows what reason.

"I told you to call me if she tries to come to work." Linc points at Hudson.

"She's not working."

I almost laugh, but I hold it together.

"We're drinking coffee," I say, holding my cup up. "Do you want me to make you some?"

Linc's gaze bounces between me and Hudson.

"It's almost five in the morning, Sadie. You should be asleep. Let's go."

"No."

"Why are you here so early?" Hudson asks him.

"I thought I could check on her and she wouldn't notice, so imagine my surprise when I see you two sitting here on your little coffee date."

I roll my eyes at my brother.

"I snuck down here, and he followed me. That's it."

"Well, let's go. You need to relax and have no stress, and this—"

"The only person adding stress to my life is you, Linc. I'm staying with Hudson."

"What?" they both ask at the same time.

"I'm not going home with you. Hudson's place is … calming."

"Calming," Hudson says with disbelief, but he's smiling.

"I'm not going to fight you, Sadie. I'll just move back to my place."

I shake my head. "For a day, and then you'll move right back in and take over again. Nope. I'm staying with Hudson."

Linc looks at his best friend, and so do I.

Hudson shrugs.

"Yeah, cool."

"Fucking unreal," Linc says and walks out.

Hudson watches him go and then looks back at me, shaking his head.

I smile. "Weird. Usually, I'm the Collins storming off in this trio, yeah?"

Hudson's deep laugh surrounds me as he stands.

"Come on, roomie, let's lock up."

I think I like being on Team Hudson.

CHAPTER TEN

HUDSON

"Hudson Asher," Linc nearly yells.

Almost everyone shifts their attention to him as he storms into the bar.

I pour a beer in front of a tourist, emerge from behind the bar, and nod toward my back office.

I knew this moment was coming.

The moment he marched his grumpy ass out of Sadie's bakery this morning, I knew he'd be coming back to talk to me without Sadie around. A simple phone call or text would have still gotten across the point he's about to make, but I understand why he wants to be here in person.

Thankfully, he waits until the door to my office is closed before he starts talking.

"What the hell, man? She's moving in with you?" He tosses his hands up, letting them drop and slap his thighs loudly.

"She's not moving in," I say and sit in my chair. "She's just staying another night or two."

Honestly, after we closed the bakery and went back to my place, she made herself at home on the sofa with a book. By the

68

time I left around ten, she was asleep on the couch. All this to say that Sadie and I haven't exactly discussed her plan.

My heart races for a split moment at the idea of her being there when I get home.

It's been years since I had someone waiting for me at the end of the day.

And now it's Sadie.

"Well, tell her to go home," Linc says, dropping into the chair opposite me. "Please."

This time, I'm the one who holds my hands up.

"I will not do that."

"Why not?"

"Because I'm keeping the peace, just like you asked."

"Don't make it sound like you're doing this for me."

"I'm not," I say and smile. "She's going to be fine, Linc. Breathe. Give her some space."

A deep wrinkle forms between his eyebrows as he leans back and glowers at me.

"Why aren't you pissed about this? It's my sister. You hate each other."

Jesus. I can't win here.

"I don't know, man. She showed up, and she was … nice."

He barks out a laugh. "To you?"

"Yes."

"Impossible."

"I thought so, too, but then I realized that if she was coming to me, she must really need a break."

His face morphs from angry to defeated in a flash.

With one hand, he rubs his forehead. "I worry about her."

"I know."

He blows out a breath.

"At least it's you. I trust you."

"Thanks."

"Dad isn't as worried. It's weird. I know he is, but he keeps saying she's just as grown a woman as she was three years ago, and she can make up her own mind on how to handle this, and I hear him, I do. I just—"

"Hey," I say, drawing his attention to me. "She's going to be fine."

I want to tell him that I know because I've been there, but again, just because I feel like I can relate to her right now doesn't mean I relate to everything. I mean, hell, a part of me wishes I didn't remember my love of hockey.

Linc needs to come to terms with his sister's accident on his own.

He nods. "Yeah. I know." He stands up quickly. "I need to get some work done. I keep pushing things off for Sadie, and I should get caught up before morning."

He moves toward the door but pauses to turn.

"You two seemed different this morning."

"Because we weren't fighting?" I laugh.

"Yeah. You almost looked at each other like …" His words trail off as he shakes his head. "I would love nothing more for you and Sadie to finally be friends."

"Oddly enough, I wouldn't be upset about that either."

He keeps his eyes on me a moment longer. I get the sense he wants to say more, but he doesn't.

He leaves, and I lean back in my seat.

Being friends with Sadie Collins sounds insane. Completely unbelievable. This town is going to lose their minds.

"Just don't get too friendly, okay?" Linc pokes his head back into my office.

"Too friendly," I repeat and stand as well because I, too, need to get back to work.

"Yeah. Too. Friendly."

"We literally just started getting along today, Linc."

He clears his throat. "Yeah, I know, I'm just worried, and the idea of you two dating and then you break up, or she gets hurt, or you get—"

"Hey, man, calm down." I slap a hand on his shoulder. "Maybe you need more sleep than your sister."

He huffs. "You might be right."

We walk side by side out of the back office. As I walk him to the front door, no one is paying attention now.

"Take care of her," Linc says, holding a hand up and walking away. He spins. "But not too much."

"Fucking get some sleep," I say with another laugh.

"I know, I know."

He unlocks his car and gets in.

I don't know which Collins to worry about more: the one who can't remember how much she hates me and decided to crash at my place or the one I've been best friends with for decades and is suddenly worried I might make a move on his sister.

I step back into the bar and spot Sadie walking in from the back. She's in different clothes now, so I assume she went back to her house to get a few things.

A few things.

So she can stay at my place.

With me.

Fuck.

She smiles and waves at me.

Betty notices, along with a couple of other regulars, and now, my worry is how the hell I'm going to pick all these jaws up off the floor.

———

"OH MY GOSH, I'm so tired," Sadie says on another yawn.

"You've been down here for hours," Betty says. "Why don't you go get some sleep? You can come to hang out with me during my shift tomorrow, too. I like having you around."

From the other side of the bar, I roll my eyes.

These two have been laughing and telling stories since Sadie walked down here to get some food. I thought she'd leave as soon as she finished eating, but she and Betty got to talking. More customers showed up, sitting at the bar. I could feel their eyes on me and wondered if word had spread that the two of us were in the same place and not fighting.

"I like it too," Luca says loudly and takes another drink of his beer.

Yep, my brother showed up, and he's been grinning like a fool since the moment he walked in.

"Yeah, I've had a good night. The best in a few days, really."

"Does your head still hurt?" Luca asks.

"Luca!" I snap.

"What?" He shrugs.

"Don't ask her that."

He grins. "It's a valid question. She hit that shit hard."

"Luca!" I scold again, this time lowering my head as I close my eyes. "Be respectful."

He laughs, and suddenly, another sound hits me. Sadie is laughing, too.

Slowly, I open my eyes to look at her.

She's watching me.

"So, let me get this straight. You're just a grump with everyone."

"Yep," Luca answers.

"Damn, I thought I was special."

"Oh, you get the worst of it by far. No one in this town gets him as worked up as you."

Oh hell.

"Luca. Aren't you done?" I ask.

"Am I talking too much?"

"Yes, you are."

"I like it," Sadie cuts in.

"Me too." This is coming from Betty. "To be honest, you're a lot less grumpy and pissed today than usual."

I open my mouth to defend myself, but Sadie speaks first.

"You would think that with his new roommate situation, he'd be a bit more in stick-up-his-butt mode."

Luca chuckles. "Hud, have a roommate? Sure okay. Who?" He sips his beer.

"Me."

And then my brother's beer sprays out of his mouth and all over Betty, who isn't even fazed.

She just smiles, moving to greet a couple of new customers as she wipes her shirt off.

"You two are living together?"

"Just briefly," I answer.

My brother's gaze bounces back and forth between us.

Then he slaps himself.

Sadie jumps back, but I just watch him.

"Are you done?"

"No. Because"—he points between us and then around the bar. He's being overly dramatic—"I have to be dreaming this. I'm sitting at a bar with you and Sadie. No one is fighting. You have both been laughing and now you live together."

As if on cue, Sadie laughs.

"Sounds about as wild as the fact that I can't remember the last three years of my life."

"Sure as shit does."

"Luca."

"What?" he says again and glares at me.

He needs to stop. She has enough on her mind. Now he's bringing it back to the memory thing, and she doesn't need that.

"I'm sorry you can't remember anything. That fucking sucks."

I'm about to tell him to get out, but I see Sadie smiling at him.

"It does fucking suck," she replies. "Really fucking sucks."

"Okay, my little foul-mouth buddies, let's dial it back."

"Okay, Dad," Luca says sarcastically.

Feeding off him, Sadie says, "Yeah, Daddy, my bad."

The three of us fall silent just then, and Luca clears his throat, tossing a twenty on the counter and getting up.

"It's really my time to leave now."

"Bye!" Sadie says to his retreating back.

"See you later," he says with a wave.

"Why don't I hang out with your brother more?" she asks me when it's just us.

"Probably because he's related to me."

She taps her nose. "That's probably true. I think I'm going to go upstairs and crash. How late do you work?"

I glance at the clock on the back wall.

"For a few more hours."

"Okay."

She hesitates and then sighs. "I need to get my wallet from my purse. I have no idea why I didn't bring it down here with me."

"Go get some sleep, Sadie. This one is on me."

She cocks her hip and crosses her arms.

"Maybe I hit my head harder than I thought because not only are we not fighting, but you also just bought me dinner."

I toss the bar towel over my schedule and lean onto my forearms, grinning.

"Are we joking about what happened already?"

She shrugs.

"Beats crying about it." She moves toward the back door. "See you in the morning, Asher."

I wink.

"See you in the morning, Collins."

She smiles and then disappears.

A throat clears behind me, and I startle.

"Jesus, Betty, where did you come from?"

"I came from the other side of the bar, but I think you forgot that there are other people in here."

"What?"

She shakes her head.

"What?" I repeat.

"Nothing."

I cross my arms. "Your face doesn't say that it's nothing."

"Okay, fine. You were clearly just flirting with Sadie."

"I was not."

"You were."

Betty has lost her mind.

"Fine. Deny it. But don't come crawling to me when you need advice."

"I won't," I say, grabbing Sadie's empty water glass and putting it in the bucket with the others that need to go to the kitchen.

First, Linc thinks I'm going to hit on her, and now Betty thinks I'm flirting.

What is wrong with everyone?

CHAPTER ELEVEN

SADIE

I made a small list of items to grab from my house yesterday, and running shoes were at the top of the list. But when I went to grab them, I couldn't find them.

So I checked the app on my phone that links with my watch to see what my current stats are and learned that I haven't run outside in months. *Months.*

Last thing I remember, I had a half marathon at the end of the summer that I've been training for.

So much for that.

I roll over in Hudson's bed.

Looks like I'll need to wait for the gym to open and then find out if I have the same locker. I bet that's where my shoes are.

It's four in the morning again, but I don't plan on sneaking down to the bakery today.

I blow out a breath.

What was my routine like?

My brain says to wake up, run, cook egg whites and spinach on gluten-free toast, and head to the bank to see if my loan for the corner space was approved.

It's all very specific.

But the corner space is now a bar—a fully functioning bar that is actually pretty nice to hang out at.

Ugh, and this apartment.

I toss the covers off and move to the window.

The bedroom view is just as amazing as the view from the balcony off Hudson's kitchen that looks over Main Street.

From this view, you can see the mountains behind the lodge, Lovers Lake at the base, and the cabins to the left. The homes in Lovers Hopefuls have almost doubled, but there weren't very many to begin with, so I guess it's okay. My small town is still small—but different.

I used to like different.

Today, not so much.

It still beats being at home, though. Sleeping and waking up in a room that's mine but isn't because I don't recognize anything in it is weird. Walking around the house looking at pictures of memories I don't have sucks. Watching my dad and brother look at me as if I am this fragile girl who might break at any moment and listening to them start a conversation around me only to cut it short because they don't want to upset me hurts. As if the only way they know how to help me is to keep me locked up. They wouldn't. Not for long, but I still can't do it.

I'd rather wake up here where the idea that it's a strange place makes sense to me. With a person whose only memories of me are … less emotionally attached.

How mad would Hudson be if I just went to the kitchen to make breakfast?

Considering he got home about four hours ago, he probably wouldn't be impressed.

I still can't believe he's back in Lovers.

I thought for sure he'd be a lifer away from this place. The talent he had for hockey was on another level. His dedication was just as intense. His parents drove him multiple nights a week to a different town for practices, and when others were spending the weekend partying, he was skating.

I think that's why I'd always told myself that if he came back, I'd make amends. I didn't think he'd ever actually do it.

I sit back on the bed, glancing around his room.

His room is bare. He doesn't have any pictures in here other than one of him with his brothers, parents, and his baby sister Ruby when she was still in a diaper.

I pick it up, and my gaze falls to his mom.

She died when he was a senior in high school. She was sick like my mom, but her cancer was more aggressive and came out of nowhere. They got her diagnosis and said their goodbyes all in five months. I spent five *years* with my mom after we found out. It doesn't make it easier, but I was luckier than him.

I set the photo down and look at my phone.

I'm still not supposed to look at it for longer than a phone call here or there, but I need to know more than Hudson told me yesterday.

I grab the phone, set a five-minute timer, and pull up the Internet.

I type his name in. It's not like he's going to burst in here and catch me, but I still hunch over as if I don't want anyone to see what I'm doing.

A few articles pop up, but I need more specifics, so I type in *Hudson Asher hockey injury*.

Another round of articles pops up, but the first headline reads *Hudson Asher Loses It All, Fame, Skill, His Team, and His Girlfriend.*

I hover my thumb over it, but then toss my phone to the end of the bed.

I know it's out there for all to read, but it's not their story to tell.

Should I try to go back to sleep or just bite the bullet and go to the bakery? I opened it for a reason. Maybe if I go back there enough, that reason will come back to me.

I pick sleeping, but just as my head hits the pillow, my alarm blares so loudly that I'm pretty sure it wakes up the entire block.

Who the hell turned that on?

My heart practically beats out of my chest as I fumble with the phone. Of course, in a moment like this, it's as if I've never used a phone in my life.

Lucky for me, even though it's a newer phone than I last remember, the manufacturer keeps the layout the same.

I blow out a breath when the beeping finally shuts off.

But then there's a knock at my bedroom door, and my heart races in a whole new way.

I open it to find a shirtless, sleepy, messy-haired Hudson on the other side, leaning on the doorframe with a yawn. It's a lot to take in, but his bright gaze hits mine, and he smirks.

"Is this going to be a daily thing?"

"What?"

"Waking up early and attempting to sneak out. Because I have to tell you, Sadie, you're not very sneaky."

I let out a bubble of laughter.

"I wasn't going to sneak out today—or well, I hadn't decided yet. I wake up, but that's not what my brain tells me to do."

He studies me for a moment.

"What does it tell you to do?"

"Wake up, work out, find a bunch of books to buy, and then research how to file a liquor license."

Now he's looking at me like I've gone mad.

"I had plans three years ago that never happened," I say to clear it up for him.

He lets out his breath.

"All right, it's still dark. Do you want to change, and we can go work out, or do you want to go to the bakery?"

"We?"

He nods. "I'm fully aware that you can do all these things on your own, but let's wait till it's been a least one-week post hospital at least, yeah?"

I want to argue, but I don't.

He's protective like my brother was, but this is different. Instead of keeping me locked up, he wants me to do what I want, just not alone.

I can compromise with that.

"Don't you want to sleep?"

His left shoulder lifts as he walks into his room, opens a dresser drawer, and takes out a shirt. He pulls it over his head and nods.

His every movement captivates me.

"I'm off today and tomorrow. I can sleep later."

"You're off all day?"

"Yeah, it's Saturday."

I suck in a breath.

Saturday.

In my head, today is Mom's funeral.

"Are you okay?" he asks, stepping toward me and bending at his knees a little to meet me at eye level. "Sadie?"

"Yes." I pull myself together. "Let's get coffees and then go work out."

"Are you sure?"

"Yes," I repeat. "I just need to change and get my shoes from the gym. When do they open?"

His eyes start at my bare legs, slowly gliding up my body. They pause briefly at my boy shorts and then again at my tank top. It's as if he hasn't noticed my outfit until this moment.

It's June in Wyoming, and it's warm out. I can't sleep with

layers, and I also didn't expect him to come in here before I put my day clothes on.

"Right. Shit. Sorry, I shouldn't have just barged in here, and they open at five."

He quickly moves to the door.

"It's your apartment, Hudson. You don't need to apologize."

He only nods, and then he walks out.

I quickly pull on some leggings and swap my tank top for a T-shirt. I brush out my hair and step into the bathroom, which has two doors: one to the bedroom and one to the living room. I wash my face, add some mascara, and brush my teeth.

When I step into the living room, Hudson is sitting on the couch, looking at his phone.

"Ready," I say.

He stands and walks to the door.

"I thought we were having coffee?" I ask.

"We are, but I don't have any here."

"What? How do you not have coffee here?"

"There is a shop right downstairs that makes way better coffee than I do."

I fold my arms and smile. "Are you complimenting me?"

"Don't let it go to your head."

I chuckle and then follow him down the stairs.

"This place really is neat. I wanted to live here once upon a time."

"Where? In Lovers?"

"No, your apartment. Last I knew, it was empty and vacant, and I was ready to move out of my parents' house."

He stops on the stairs to turn and look at me.

I can't decipher the gaze he gives me, but the wrinkle between his eyes says he's thinking a little too hard.

But I don't say anything else, and he shakes his head, and we make our way to the bakery.

I let us in, and we make coffee. I don't get as emotional as I did yesterday, but even as we hang out, nothing comes back to me on why I did this.

Why would I choose the bakery over my own dream?

"Ready?" Hudson asks, handing me my coffee.

"Would I bask in this?"

"In what?"

"You serving me instead of the other way around?"

He lets out a deep laugh.

"Oh, yeah."

"Good."

Our eyes meet, and I can't help but decide that I like being friends with him a lot more than I like fighting.

We walk out the back door, and Hudson turns left.

"Isn't the gym this way?"

"We aren't going to the gym."

"What? I thought we were working out."

"We are going for a walk first."

He's steps ahead of me, so I jog a little in my flats to catch up.

Just Sadie and Hudson, walking down Main Street, sipping their coffee.

I giggle.

"I'm thinking it, too," Hudson says. "It's probably good that the sun is just now coming up, and most people aren't awake yet."

"They'd be taking photos like we were royalty walking around. So," I start and catch him shaking his head. "What?"

"You talk a lot."

"Me?"

"Yes."

"You knew that, though."

"No, I knew we fought a lot, and you always had to have the last word, but you like just talking in general. "

"Or maybe I'm just trying to make up for lost time."

"I'll give you that."

I have so many things I want to ask him, but I don't. I'm not silent now because he said something about it; I'm just not sure what to say first.

What do we fight the most about? What's it like being back? Did his girlfriend try to move here with him? Does he still skate? Why didn't I open my own business?

There are more things I want to know, but those are at the top of the list.

The silence that settles between us isn't weird. It feels natural, as if I've been hanging out with him my entire life. In a way, I have, but I'm starting to wonder if I missed out.

When we reach the end of the road, he slows, then picks some flowers from Mrs. Rogers's rosebushes.

"What are you doing?"

"We need flowers," he says matter-of-factly.

"For what?"

He points ahead of us with the red roses in his hand. "Your mom."

My gaze snaps to the cemetery. I hadn't even noticed this was where we were walking.

Tears fill my eyes.

"In your mind, you were going to say goodbye to her today, so it makes sense that you come to see her and tell her everything you wanted to say back then."

He hands me the flowers. "You buy much nicer ones, but you leave these from time to time from here."

I swallow the lump in my throat.

"Hudson, this …"

"Fuck, I didn't mean to make you cry. I just thought you might like to—*shit*, I don't know."

I let out what sounds like a laugh-cry mixture. "It's perfect."

I take the flowers from him, and he leads the way. He shows me which one is her stone, and then he takes a few steps back to give me privacy. He walks down another row. That one, I know, has his mom.

When he's far enough away not to hear me, I squat in front of Mom's gravestone and lay the flowers down, swapping them with faded and dry ones.

I let myself cry for a moment. How do I do this? What do I say?

Hudson made it sound like I come here often. How often?

I clear my throat.

"I have so much I want to tell you," I whisper. "But right now, even when I should be focusing on myself and trying to regain my memory, I can think of only one thing."

I smile.

"You'd be so proud, Mom. I did it. I finally became friends with Hudson."

CHAPTER TWELVE

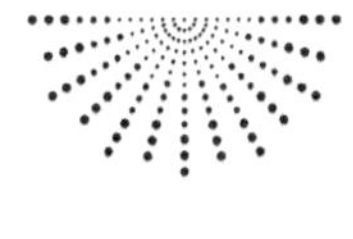

HUDSON

It's official. I'm buying a new couch.

I sit up with a groan and then rub my lower back.

I hate sleeping during the day, but after I woke up with Sadie, I knew I would be trying to catch up on a few hours as soon as we got back.

I twist to look back at the bedroom. The door is wide open, and from the angle I can see, the bed is made too. The kitchen is empty, and the bathroom light is off.

Sadie isn't here.

We still need to discuss her plans for staying here, but this morning wasn't the time.

I already know I'm going to let her stay as long as she wants.

Which is completely nuts.

I chuckle and drop my head to the back of the sofa.

If you had asked two weeks ago—hell, even a week ago—if I ever thought I could be friends with her, I'd have laughed in your face.

Look at us now.

I push to stand. My leg feels stiffer than usual, so I take a couple of minutes to do some stretches. I'm just finishing up when my phone buzzes.

There's no missing the red circle with a sixteen inside it next to my text messages.

I open it quickly to see a group chat between Linc, Luca, Miles, and myself.

As kids, Linc and I didn't hang out with Luca and Miles a lot. We are three years apart. But as adults, these are the guys I'd trust with my life.

LINC

Has anyone seen Hudson today?

MILES

Nope. Why?

LUCA

He was closing the bar last night. He's probably still asleep.

LINC

Okay. I just wanted to check in on my sister.

MILES

Why would Hud have that answer?

LUCA

Oh shit, you don't know, do you?

MILES

Know what?

LUCA

Hud and Sadie are living together.

MILES

... no.

LINC

> She's staying with him because she's mad
> at me.

MILES

> What is today?

LUCA

> It's not April's Fools, bro. It's a true story.

THE REST of the messages are about the same. Their discussion on my personal life. I click over to a thread for just Linc and I.

LINC

> How is she today? I'd text her, but I don't want
> her on her phone—you know, screens.

I ROLL my eyes and grin at his lame attempt to hover. I know she can't use screens, but I don't think a quick text reply is going to do a whole lot of damage.

Then again, I'm not a doctor, so what do I know?

I shower quickly and head downstairs for some lunch.

Since owning a bar, I rarely eat at home. It doesn't help that Sadie's coffee shop is right there, too.

Who knows, maybe I'll buy a coffee pot when I buy a new couch.

The lunch rush is gone by the time I walk in, so it's quiet enough for me to hear her laughter from the moment I open the door to the kitchen.

"Hey, Boss," Mickey, my kitchen manager, says as I walk in.

"Hey, how's it going in here?"

"Good. It was another busy day."

"That's good. Where's Ian?" I ask. Ian is the other kitchen employee. Together, they are an unmatched duo. I'm lucky to have them working for me.

"On break."

"Make sure you get one too."

"I will. What are you having today?"

"Let's do the crispy chicken salad."

He smiles and nods. "I just made one for Miss Sadie out there. She's something else."

She sure is.

"Good. Make sure she gets anything she wants."

"You got it," he says and gets to work.

I make my way to the front, and right there, with a crowd around her, is Sadie. The men sitting on either side of her are my brothers.

"I swear, I had no idea you were this funny," Miles says.

"I told you. We missed out on so much because of her hate for Huddy."

"Huddy," Sadie repeats.

What the hell are these two doing? Hitting on her?

Shit. And Linc was worried about me.

"Don't you two have something better to do than hang out here every day?" I ask a little louder than normal to make my presence known.

Both of my brothers turn to look at me with giant grins, but it's Sadie who steals my focus. She's wearing a light blue summer dress and white shoes, with her hair braided down the back. She smiles at me, the flecks in her gaze drinking me in.

"I thought you'd never wake up."

"Were you waiting for me?"

"Yes."

I step behind the bar and make myself an ice water. When I'm done, I take the seat on the other side of Miles. I want to tell him to get up so I can sit by Sadie, but why do I need to do that? Why do I have this urge to be the one she sits next to?

"You're not even going to ask her why she was waiting for you?" Luca prods.

I look at Sadie. "Why were you waiting for me?"

"I got you something."

My left brow rises as I keep my gaze on her. Is this a real gift, or is she going to play a prank on me?

"Stop looking at me like that," she says, rolling her eyes and getting off her stool. She walks behind my brother and sand- wiches herself between us to lean on the bar top.

Her breasts brush against my right biceps, and even though I have to swallow back my next gulp, I pretend I don't notice.

"It won't be here till Monday, but do you want to know what it is?"

"Do I?"

Sadie frowns and then looks at my brothers. "Why is his face doing that?"

Luca barks out a laugh while Miles shakes his head.

"I think he's confused about the ray of sunshine that you are today. He isn't sure how to respond."

"Stop, all of you," I say.

"See,"—Miles points at me—"grump." He points at Sadie. "Sunshine. He definitely doesn't know what to do right now."

Mickey brings me my salad, so I ignore my brothers and take the first bite. Once I swallow, I look at Sadie. "Tell me my surprise."

"Oh, you just needed food. Noted."

Then she pulls out her phone.

I groan.

"Your brother would kill me if he knew you're playing on that thing."

She leans in close. "Well then, I guess we won't tell him, will we?" she whispers.

A feeling that I haven't felt in years sprints through me. It reminds me of when I tested my dad's dog's shock collar with my finger. A zap of electricity brings me back to life. My heart pounds and my dick stirs at the feel of her warm breath against my ear.

"Besides, all I did was look this up and order it."

She holds her phone out in front of me.

"Why are you showing me a picture of a couch?"

"Because," she says proudly, "I bought it for you."

"You bought me a couch?"

I grab the phone from her and examine it, swiping through the pictures. It's longer than the one I have now, and it pulls out to double the size. It looks easy to switch back and forth from bed to couch. It could totally work if—oh shit.

"How long do you plan on staying with me?"

"That"—she holds her finger up as she sets her phone face down on the counter—"is a very good question. We should talk about that, but that isn't why I did it. It's twofold, really. One, your couch sucks, and two, this morning was ... it was ... really meaningful to me."

Her eyes start to gloss over just as Luca says, "What did you two do this morning?"

"Yes, do tell," Miles adds.

Fuck. I'd forgotten they were here.

That anyone was here, really.

"Hudson took me to visit my mom's grave. He knew my

brain said today was her funeral, so he took me there to say goodbye. Again, I guess."

"No shit," Luca says.

I take another bite as both brothers watch me.

"Anyway, I've been down here long enough. When you're done eating, we can talk about our plan for the next few weeks."

She hugs Luca and then Miles and heads for the back.

Not one second after the door closes, my brothers start in on me.

"You took her to see her mom?" Luca asks first.

"It's not that big of a deal."

"It is though," Miles says.

"It's not."

"Hud, look, I mean this in the nicest way possible, but you've been a selfish prick since you came back."

Jesus.

"No, I haven't."

"Um, yes, you have. We invite you to do things all the time, and the only time you come is if Dad asks. You don't do anything but work here, work out, and sit in your apartment. You just take care of yourself. Only you."

"I don't say no all the time."

It's a pathetic response to defend myself, because I know they aren't wrong. I don't see the point in having hopes, dreams, or goals anymore. They can vanish in a heartbeat. Keeping to myself means I can't be disappointed.

"Our opinions stand, but the point is," Luca says, "you did something for someone else—for Sadie—something extra meaningful."

I sigh, going back to my lunch.

When did these two get so sappy?

"It wasn't a big deal."

"It might not have been for you, but for her, it was. For us, it is."

They both stand, tossing some cash onto the bar.

"We'll talk later," Miles says, and they leave.

I let their words play over in my mind while I eat.

I care about other people. I do.

I just have a different way of showing it.

I finish my lunch and head back upstairs. Music is playing when I open the door, and Sadie is in the kitchen.

She pauses, turning her focus from inside one of the cupboards to me.

She smiles, and I swear my heart skips at the sight of her greeting me when I get home.

"Hypothetically, if one wanted you to say yes to a question, what kind of baked goods would one need to provide in order for that to happen?"

I chuckle.

"What's your question?"

She closes the cabinet and walks toward me.

I normally dread her approach, but today, I look forward to hearing what she says.

She sighs. "I really feel like my chances are better if I have treats."

"Sadie, ask me whatever you want."

"All right, let's sit, though."

"Sit? Is it that bad?"

She grabs my hand, pulls me to the couch, and pushes me down to sit. I imagine her crawling over me and sitting on my lap with one leg on each side and pressing her body flush against me, but instead she sits next to me, and the moment is gone.

What the fuck is wrong with me?

"Can I stay here until … well, until I'm ready to go home?"

"Are we being transparent here?"

"Of course."

"How long will that be?"

"I don't know."

"If Linc moved out, why won't you go back home?"

She wrinkles her nose as she thinks over her words.

"They remember the last few years. I don't. They have pictures, memories, and things that … hurt when I see them. I'll have to go back eventually, but I need time to come to terms with it. That place seems foreign to me now, and even my room is different."

"My apartment is unfamiliar to you."

"Yes, but the difference is that it makes sense why this place is that way."

"Why did you pick me? You could have gone anywhere else."

"True. But you don't make me feel like I just woke in a hospital. You make me feel like you're not waiting for me to remember everything right this second. Like I can take my time and figure it out on my own."

Her words hit me hard. I needed that person after my injury. I thought I had her, too, in my girlfriend at the time, but she left. Turns out she wasn't with me for me—she liked the fame and name that I gave her more.

"You can stay here as long as you need to, Sadie. There's no rush."

"Thank you."

She hesitates.

"Is that all?"

"No."

"Okay," I chuckle. "Rip off the Band-Aid."

"Will you help me get through this and hopefully remember?"

Her question takes me by surprise, so I lean back.

"How?"

"I don't know yet."

I nod slowly. Well, this sounds easy. But, like I said, I didn't have anyone there for me. I won't saddle Sadie with that same fate.

It hurt too much, and even though our past is nothing but one big fight, I won't let her go through it alone.

If she wants my help, she's got it.

CHAPTER THIRTEEN

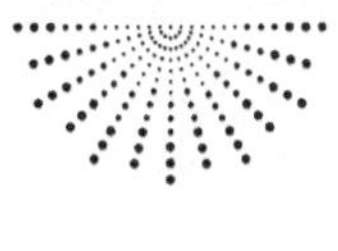

SADIE

"Is this what you do every day?" I ask as we sit in Hudson's living room.

He's reading more of his thriller book, and I'm bored out of my mind. Now, I know I said I wanted him to help me remember, but I'm pretty sure staying inside won't help. It's a beautiful day outside. We should be doing something.

"Let's go," I say and stand, rounding the back of the couch to put on some shorts. "Give me five minutes."

"Where are we going?"

"I'm not sure yet."

"Sounds fun."

"Gosh," I say, leaving his bedroom door cracked so he can hear me. "You really are a grump."

"I'm not a grump," he defends himself. "I just like what I like. There's a difference."

I slip my shorts on. They are spandex underneath but loose and flowy on the outside. I change into a crop top and grab a jacket.

"Okay, I'm ready."

Hudson stands, his lips parting as if he's going to say something, but he stops. His hands rest on his hips, and he scowls at me.

"What kind of outfit is that?"

"This?" I look down. "A comfy one?"

He looks down at his jeans and shirt. As far as I can remember, I've never seen him wear anything else.

"Should I change?"

"No. Let's just stroll through town. You can tell me what I missed."

He studies me for a moment and then nods.

We lock up, cross through the bar, and step out onto Main Street.

"Which way should we go?" I ask.

"Left," he says and starts walking.

The door to the space between his bar and my bakery opens, and Mrs. Whittaker steps out.

"Oh, damn. I don't have time for you two right now."

"Good afternoon, Mrs. Whittaker. How are you?" I ask, and she freezes.

Her gaze snaps to Hudson.

He shrugs.

Her focus returns to me with a sigh. "I heard about what happened. How are you?"

"I'm fine. Thank you. It's been a crazy few days, but Hudson is helping me, so all is well."

"Hudson is what?" she asks. She even takes a step forward and turns her head to the side as if she needs to hear me better.

"He's helping me."

Her bottom lip drops as she looks at us as if she just saw a ghost.

"Well, we are on a stroll, so we can chat later," Hudson chimes in. He leads me around her.

I peek over my shoulder; she hasn't moved.

"Do you think she's okay?"

"She's fine, but I have a feeling we're going to see a lot of that while we're out and about."

And he's not wrong.

We pause in front of a dance studio, which, last I remember, was a pottery store. Hudson tells me about the woman who opened it and how it's been a hit with the guests of Lovers Lodge. Then we stop in front of Mrs. Simmer's coffee hut. It turns out that, last year, Mr. Simmer gave coffee away free for a whole day, and she locked him out of their house for two nights.

We stop in front of a few more places, but nothing else changed overall. That's what I love about small towns. The only difference today is the look of shock as people spot us.

We reach the mechanic shop, and Miles steps out, wiping his hands on a rag.

"Hey," he says. "Fancy seeing you two just taking a walk together."

"We're trying to see if I remember anything by walking around town and looking at familiar things."

"Is it helping?"

I shake my head. "The only thing I wish I could remember right now was that Paige King stayed at the lodge and ran out on her own wedding. Oh, I bet the town loved that. The gossip must have been unhinged."

Miles chuckles, and so does Hudson.

I glance over at my new roommate.

I like it when he laughs.

I like how deep it is and how, when I hear it, it creates a flutter in my stomach. I want to make him laugh more.

Which is absolutely insane.

How hard did I hit my head?

"Well, did Huddy tell you that her new fiancé's best friend is Mrs. Bank's grandson?"

"Seriously?"

Miles nods.

"They did a signing here last summer at the lodge, and she came with him."

"And I missed it. Dang it!"

The brothers share a look, and then Hudson clears his throat.

"If I remember right, Linc took your picture with her. She came to the bakery every morning they were here."

"Oh."

"Well, we better get going," Hudson says quickly. His hand bumps my lower back as he nudges me along. We make it about ten steps when I notice he's limping.

"Are you okay? Did you step off the sidewalk weird or something?" I ask, pointing to his leg.

"No, I'm fine."

"You don't look fine."

"I'm fine."

"Hudson, don't do that with me."

"Do what, Sadie? Argue? That's what we do."

I take a deep breath, turn to face him, and stop him in his tracks.

"No. I refuse to let you start a fight. I know it's weird that we suddenly get along, but that's who we are now. Now, you either tell me why you're limping, or I can look it up online. Your choice."

He sighs.

"It's just a flare-up. It happens when I'm more active than normal."

"Oh, well, let's go sit down then. That wasn't that hard."

"Right, because every woman wants to hear that the man

she's with needs to sit down because his leg hurts when they're in their thirties."

I laugh lightly, taking a seat on the bench right across the street from his bar.

He sits, too, and I can hear his breath letting go the moment the pressure is off his leg.

"Good for you that I'm only—*noooooo.*"

I suck in a breath and cover my mouth with my hands.

Without moving them, I say, "I turn thirty in a few weeks."

Hudson starts to chuckle and then cuts himself off with a closed fist to his lips.

"Yes, you do."

"Oh my god. Oh. My. God."

Tears start to sting my eyes.

When they fall, there is no controlling them. I expect Hudson to comment that crying still bothers him, but instead, he wraps a hand around my shoulders and pulls me close. This time, he doesn't tell me to stop.

"I was beginning to think you were too calm over all this," he says softly.

"Denial is real." I inhale. "Everything seems the same, but it's not. It all looks the same, but on the inside, it's not. How am I supposed to deal with this?"

"One day at a time," he answers quickly. "Just one day at a time."

I'm unsure how long we sit together, but we stay here until my stomach growls. Then we go back to his apartment to make grilled chicken and sweet potatoes. After, we watch a movie and fall asleep on the couch.

I might not have remembered anything new today, but I will remember today.

And I owe it all to Hudson.

CHAPTER FOURTEEN

HUDSON

I woke up before Sadie today. She was still asleep when I left for the gym.

I needed the space.

It's not that I don't enjoy having her around.

I do, which I see as a problem.

Especially after my body reacted to her at the bar yesterday.

It's almost as if all the emotions I had toward her turned from annoyance and fight into … hell, into the complete opposite.

She was the first thing on my mind when I woke up today. Not the bar, not the fact that my life wasn't the way I planned, not that I was back in Lovers, not … normal.

Instead, I wondered if I should wake her to get breakfast, ask whether we should take another walk around town to see if today brings something back to her or see if she just wanted to be awake with me because I like being around her.

So I grabbed some gym clothes and left.

I can't even be mad, because I feel different today. Almost as if I woke up actually looking forward to something.

It reminds me a little of game day. The thrill of what the day will bring. Am I going to win, or will I leave knowing I need to do better next time?

There is nothing sad about my mental state today, and that's refreshing.

I press the button for more resistance on the bike.

My leg was bugging me first thing this morning, so instead of dwelling on why, I decided to do something about it.

Sadie wants to be proactive in remembering her life. She asked for my help, but even if she hadn't, she would have done it on her own.

She's choosing to stay positive in a hard time.

I should have chosen that path. Instead, I chose anger and resentment. I chose to shut people out. Being around Sadie has made my brain think differently.

An hour later, I'm walking back to my apartment when I spot the light on in the bakery.

I move to the front window and spot Sadie sitting at one of the tables. She's got a notepad in front of her as she taps a pen to her lips.

Her pink, plump lips spread into a smile when she sees me.

I clear my throat, trying not to show how much I enjoy what that smile is doing to me.

"Hey, stranger," she says and opens the door.

I step in, and she locks it behind me.

"Morning. I'm glad to see you slept in today."

"Yeah, well, the first place I still went to was down here."

"Did you start baking again?"

She shakes her head.

"Can I tell you a secret?"

I eye her. She twists her lips and bites her fingernail as she waits for me to reply.

"Sure."

"You can't tell Linc or my dad."

I nod and then take a seat. "The secrets are stacking up, Sadie."

"I know."

"But let's hear it."

I don't especially like the idea of hiding anything from her brother, but if it helps her, I'll do it.

"I don't like baking."

I don't say anything right away. I think she's letting her words sink in as much as I am.

"My mom," she goes on, "loved this place, and I'm starting to think that I only kept it going because of that."

"Is that what you want now?"

"I don't know." she groans. "It's clearly doing well, but I can't stop thinking about Sips and Stories, and everything is just confusing."

"Sips and Stories?"

She smiles. It's different from the one she usually gives me, but it's all the more amazing.

"Yes. I was going to open it where your bar is, with a corner window reading spot. It was going to be filled with flowers and a bar in the back for fun dunks. There would be big cloud chairs and sofas all around where people could sit and read. They would bring their own books or get one off the shelves. A mimosa and a romance novel in a room full of flowers just sounds so ... soothing."

I've never heard her so enthusiastic about something. She sure as hell didn't sound this passionate when she made her pitch to Mrs. Whittaker ten days ago.

I bought the bar through email before I moved back. I had no idea she wanted it.

The bar space and the apartment.

Shit.

I stole her dream right after her mom had passed away.

I wouldn't have tried to make amends with me, either.

"You think it's stupid, don't you?"

"No, why would you think that?"

"You're just sitting there in silence."

I blow out a breath.

"I'm thinking that I have a hunch on why you hated me so much when I came back."

"Yeah?"

"Yeah. I bought the bar. I took your dream, and so you made a new one." I gesture to the bakery.

"You think so?"

"It makes sense. You've hated me even more than usual since I came back."

Our eyes lock, and she bites her lip.

Oh hell. The urge to yank her chair toward me so that my mouth can replace hers hits me hard. My hand even twitches.

"What's this?" I ask to change the subject quickly. I tap on her notepad.

"Oh, it's all my questions for why I'm doing what I do now."

"Let's hear them."

She laughs. "Well, number eight is, has Hudson always been this sweet?"

I bark out a laugh.

"I'm not sweet."

"You're pretty sweet."

The things my mind wants to do her right now are anything but sweet. On this table, with her stripped bare for the entire town to see through the front window.

"I think we will have to agree to disagree. What else is on there?"

"Okay, I have, why do I own the bakery? Why do I still live with my dad? Did I date anyone in the last few years? Who is my best friend now, and where are they? What are my hobbies now?

And why was I at the bakery that afternoon? Maybe if I knew what I was doing, it would bring something back."

A lump forms in my throat. I have no way to prove it, but I think she was there because of me.

An ache hits my chest.

Do I tell her that? How much do I share with her? My gut tells me that she'd want to know everything and anything that would help her remember even the slightest detail at this point, but my heart says to wait until I know for sure.

I clear my throat and nod to the kitchen. "Have you baked anything since you woke up in the hospital?"

She shakes her head and looks down as if she's ashamed to admit it.

"Maybe start there."

She looks up, her gaze landing on me for a fleeting moment before she stares at the kitchen door.

"I used to bake with my mom, but it was just for fun. It wasn't ever something I would want to make into a career, or so I thought. Jeez, listen to me. I'm like a broken record. You know all this."

"Hey, don't be so hard on yourself. Maybe if you bake something that your mom and you did together, something will come back. Who knows—maybe you kept this place going as a way to stay close to her."

I look around at all the tables she has and the pictures from over the years and then to the glass hutch where she usually keeps the day's freshest baked goods. It's weird to look at it this way. Empty.

After a minute passes, I return my focus to Sadie, who is just watching me.

"What?" I ask.

Her gaze narrows. "I'm just trying to figure out how I missed all this."

"Missed what?"

"You. Moments like just now make me feel like I never really knew you."

I shrug. "Maybe you didn't."

She nods slowly and moves to the kitchen.

"I think I'll take your advice. My mom's favorite thing to make were lemon bars. I have her recipe memorized, and they are melt-in-your-mouth amazing."

I try to keep my expression neutral. It's hard.

The ache in my chest returns.

"I'll let you get to it, then." I turn to the door, ready to get some fresh air.

Is this all really a good idea?

What happens when she remembers why she was here?

What if I was, in fact, the reason?

My hand is on the door handle when she stops me.

"Do you want to bake with me?"

I freeze, then slowly turn and rub the back of my neck.

"I'm, uh…"

She waves a hand in front of her face. "I'm sorry. Ignore me. Just because my life is weird right now doesn't mean you should abandon yours. I'll see you later."

I can't quite place the look on her face. Defeat, maybe? Or maybe it's more of what I imagine someone who is attempting to put on a brave face would look like.

Is she worried about being here alone again?

She was here by herself when I found her, but that doesn't mean she wasn't worried.

The rest of my day plays out quickly in my head: shower, dress, eat lunch at the bar, and then go back to my apartment to do whatever my mind comes up with.

Another typical day in the life of Hudson Asher.

So, of course, I do what every man in my shoes would do.

"You know what? I think I'll stay."

Her head snaps up, and the way her face lights up tells me I made the right choice.

"Oh, yay. You're going to love these bars."

Oh, I know I will. They are the best thing she makes.

I'll be sure to tell her the truth this time.

CHAPTER FIFTEEN

SADIE

"Do you think we made too many?" I ask, taking a step back from the counter. I place my hands on my hips and look at our end product.

Hudson, too, steps back, his elbow brushing mine to mimic my stance as he looks at the counter with me.

"You know, I think the fact we made enough for us to live off these for a few months might make the answer to your question *yes, yes we did.*"

"Hmmm. I was sure the third batch would bring something back to my memory."

It's not a lie. I did feel something while we were baking. It just wasn't what I thought it would be.

"Nothing worked?"

I shake my head and then grin at him, letting a small laugh loose.

"What?"

"You still have powdered sugar everywhere."

I reach up to swipe some off his cheek. I had high hopes that I'd remember something through baking, but all I felt was happy and relaxed, as if I never hit my head and have three years unaccounted for. My company in the kitchen was no doubt the reason for that.

Hudson listened carefully to me, and he did everything he was told, cracking jokes or reminding me of moments he saw me baking with my mom as a kid.

This afternoon just felt … good.

I like that Hudson was here with me.

"It's like you've never baked before," I say and start to put the endless buffet of lemon bars into boxes. "Should we donate these?"

"Or you could sell them," he says coolly. "I'm sure if you saved them for tomorrow, people would still come rushing in to buy them, even if that's all you have."

I pause. It makes perfect sense. I own a bakery, for crying out loud. I should do it.

It just feels wrong to sell them. It's almost like the idea of making money off these would ruin the joy they gave me. Giving them away, on the other hand—that makes me smile.

"Maybe next time," I say. After all, until last week, selling them is what I did. "Let's give these bars away."

"Miles and Luca would love to take some, if we are just picking randoms."

"My dad and brother too. Maybe even Betty."

"And Brooke," Hudson adds.

I don't know why, but his suggestion to give these to another woman surprises me. Does he like Brooke?

"Brooke Sloan?" I ask.

He nods.

"Oh, are you two …"

He tilts his head as he looks at me. "You've stayed with me for three nights now. If I had a girlfriend, I would have told you by this point."

"Oh" is all I say.

"I suggested Brooke since she works with you, and as far as I know, she's your only friend. You can cross that off your list of questions."

"What?" I say with a laugh. "Brooke works for me?"

"For almost two years now."

I grab my phone from my back pocket immediately and scroll through my contacts. I tap her name since it's at the top of the contacts list and open up a message thread with her. It instantly brings up where our last conversation left off the morning of my accident.

"Why do you think she hasn't reached out?" I ask before I type anything.

"She's been out of town for her sister's wedding. Plus, were you friends the last you remember? Maybe she was scared."

"I mean, we said hi in passing."

"There you have it."

I twist my lips and look down at our messages.

We talk about books and wine dates and clothes, and there seems to a lot of chatter about firemen. And lots of emojis.

The last one she sent contains water drops, a fireman, a firework, and then a bed. It's almost like code text.

What does that mean?

"Do I have a crush on anyone?" I ask aloud.

"How would I know?"

Hudson is cleaning up now, wiping down the counters and putting some dishes in the sink. He keeps looking at the bars, though.

"Did you eat one?" I ask.

"Not yet."

"Well, let's grab one." I push a box toward him as I contemplate what I could text to Brooke.

What must it feel like to have your best friend forget you?

My heart hurts for her, so I quickly send a text.

SADIE

Hey :) How are you?

"DID YOU TEXT HER?" Hudson asks right before he takes a bite. The moan that follows distracts me from replying to his question. His eyes are closed, and he's nodding with a smile. I feel the deep sound that escapes him all the way to my toes.

MY PHONE BUZZES before I speak.

BROOKE

Hi! I'm good. I just got home this morning. How are you? I know it's a silly question, but yeah.

SADIE

I'm good. It's not a silly question. Do you want to have dinner soon?

HUDSON MOANS AGAIN. My heart pulses and my palms grow clammy. I watch his lips and then his throat as it bobs when he swallows. Holy hell, I've never been so turned on watching someone eat before.

BROOKE

Yes. Do you want to come over tonight? Or I
can come to you.

AFTER THE THIRD MOAN, I reply:

SADIE

Your place is great. Remind me of the address.

SHE TYPES IT BACK, and I pretend I don't hear Hudson when he
goes for another bar. Dinner can't come soon enough, because
boy oh boy, do I have questions for Brooke.

———

BROOKE IS WAITING at the door when I arrive at her house.

It's part of a duplex two blocks over from Main Street.

She smiles and waves.

"Hi." I smile back. "I have so many questions."

She lets out a small laugh.

"So do I, but I'm not sure you're going to have answers to
mine."

I hate that I don't remember the friendship we've built in the
last two years, but on the other hand, I grew up with Brooke, so
the moment I walk into her house, I feel a sense of familiarity.
The smell of apples and cinnamon surrounds me, and even
though no memories come back, my shoulders relax.

It smells like her. Maybe coming here will be better than I thought.

"I ordered pizza," she says quickly. "I also bought stuff to make mimosas, but I'm not sure you can drink. I should have thought of that."

"Mimosas and pizza? Is that a thing?"

She hesitates. "For us, it is."

I love how she says *is* and not *was*.

I nod and walk right into her kitchen. "One drink won't hurt. Plus, I walked here."

We sit at the table and fix our plates. I expect silence to fill the room, but Brooke clearly has other plans.

"I can't believe your brother let you walk. Alone."

"He didn't. I'm staying with Hudson for a while."

She pauses with her pizza halfway to her mouth.

"I heard that, but I didn't really believe it," she says. She takes a bite and chews slowly.

"So, what's it like living with the sworn enemy?"

I love how she asks it as if … as if this is just another day for her, and we are just picking up where we left off. Like we are best friends. Which we are, of course.

My heart swells.

"Well"—I take a giant bite—"have we ever talked about his abs?"

Brooke erupts into a fit of laughter. "We have, but you usually talk about them with disgust. I have a feeling that's not the case today."

"It's not." I relax back into my chair. "It's definitely not."

"So, are you two becoming friends now?"

"I think so. I hope so."

This time, her smile is sly.

"What's that face? I should probably know what it means, but you know, I don't."

Her smile falters for a fleeting moment, but then grows into a full-fledged grin. "Wait here."

She dashes from the room, and I twist to see where she went, but she's out of sight. I finish my slice before she makes it back.

She drops about ten books on the table and then sits.

"Okay, we don't really have to talk about what happened to you if you don't want to. It sucks. Pure sucks. I've missed you, and I'm sorry I didn't reach out. I didn't think you'd remember our friendship, and I wanted you to have space from everyone expecting you to remember them."

I stick my bottom lip out because the way she's looking at me makes me want to cry.

I lean forward to hug her. "I don't, but twenty minutes here, and I already know that I'd pick you over and over again."

Her eyes start to glaze, and so do mine.

"Okay, I won't cry, but I'd pick you too."

Before we become two crying messes, I point to the books. "Are these your favorites?"

She tosses her head back on a groan, but when she looks at me, she's still smiling. "This is going to sound so messed up, but a reader's dream is to read their favorite books for the first time all over again, and you get to do that." She taps the pile. "These are all your favorite enemies-to-lovers books over the last few years. Oddly enough, it's your favorite trope these days."

"They are?" I grab the one off the top and read the blurb. A male romance writer who marries his enemy in Vegas, and she just so happens to be his best friend's little sister. "Oh, this sounds good."

"That's why it's on the top. Take them with you. Enjoy reading them again while you can."

"Don't I have copies at home?"

"Probably, but you prefer e-books, and Linc said you shouldn't look at a screen more than necessary for a while."

I nod. "Do you talk to my brother a lot?"

She shakes her head. "He called to check in on me and kept me up to date on some things while I was gone."

"That was nice of him."

"Of your brother or Hudson for letting you live with him?"

"Both." I reach for more pizza. "Hudson is also helping me try to get my memory back."

"Willingly? Like he wants you to remember that you hate him?"

"Hate is such a strong word." I cringe. "The last thing I remember about him was that he was playing hockey, and I swore I'd mend things between us if he ever came back, but it turns out I didn't."

"Of course not. Your bags were basically packed to move into the place Hudson now calls home, but then they sold the space practically overnight to someone who offered them cash, above value, overnight. Cue Hudson's Bar."

"Ouch. So that really is what happened. He thought as much when we talked about it earlier today."

She nods. "To his credit, he had no idea you were trying to buy it first."

"And I was still mad at him?"

"Mad?" she laughs. "Honey, you downright put him on your shitlist the day he came back."

I sigh. "I don't sound like a nice person where he's concerned."

She reaches over to cover my hand. "You're the sweetest. Your relationship with Hudson has always been different, even now."

He's been amazing, and it makes me feel bad how I've acted.

"Oh my gosh, I've never seen you smile that way before," Brooke says, kicking me gently with her foot. "Are you thinking of him?"

"Who?" I play dumb.

She rolls her eyes. "Hudson."

I scrunch my nose and feel my cheeks warming.

"Am I crazy? I mean, he's been really great since this all happened. Maybe I'm overthinking that."

"No way. This is good. I like this for you. In the time we started this friendship and have worked together, you've never once shown interest in any guy."

"I haven't? Well, that answers one of my questions. I was wondering when the last time I had sex was."

I slap my hand over my lips the moment the words are out of my mouth. Mumbling, I say, "I'm so sorry. That was too much information."

"You told me about your first blow job, so it's really not. And unless you're keeping secrets from me, the last time you slept with anyone was last summer with this rich asshole who was here for a wedding at the lodge."

"I had a fling?"

"You had a fling." She nods. "Honestly, I think you might have made it last the entire weekend he was here, but he was kicked out of Hudson's bar, so he didn't really leave the lodge after that."

"Why? What did he do?"

She shrugs. "I have no clue. Can I ask you something on a different subject?"

"Go for it." I settle in, ready to broach another topic.

"Are you going to reopen the bakery, or should I look for another job?"

Oh.

I haven't really thought about it, and it never really occurred to me that I was putting others out of a paycheck.

I stare at the table as I finally think about it.

"Do you bake, too?" I ask.

She nods. "You've taught me everything you know."

"Do you think you could run it without me for a bit?"

It's not that I don't want to go back. It's just weird. Being there and not having a passion for it.

"I could, yeah, but it's more fun with you."

"I don't doubt that—friends do have more fun, but maybe for just a few weeks."

"I can do that."

We spend the next two hours talking about the lodge and the tourists who have come through the town. She tells me about the summer festival last year and how this year's will take place in a couple weeks. The bakery has an event, but she promises she can handle it without me and assures me she has a new recipe she wants everyone to try.

By the time I'm walking up the steps to Hudson's apartment, I know the exact reason why Brooke and I fit so well.

She has a passion for baking that reminds me of my mother. I have no doubt that's how we bonded and became best friends.

I push the door open slowly. It's dark inside beyond the TV screen glow. Hudson sits up as I close the door behind me.

"Hey, I wasn't sure when you'd be back." He stands, wincing as he stretches his leg.

"Why don't you sleep in your room until the new couch is here? It should be delivered tomorrow."

"I'm not sleeping in my room, Sadie. You keep the bed. What's in the bag?" He points to the lily-covered gift bag filled with books in my hand.

"My favorite novels, it seems. Brooke sent them with me."

"Did you have fun?"

"I did. I learned a lot."

I set the bag down and cross my arms.

Hudson's eyes take in the motion slowly before mimicking my action and looking me in the eye.

It's like he's preparing to spar with me.

"What did you learn?" he asks.

"Well, first off, you bought the bar out from under me and moved in here, and that's why I don't own it right now."

He nods.

"So I was right?"

"Don't gloat." I shove his arm.

"I'm not."

He's smirking.

"Why have you never told me this? Or why didn't you mention it sooner?"

I'm not really mad, but it would have helped, I think.

He shrugs. "I didn't think it mattered. I only put it together today, and it would have been from my view. I didn't think it was fair to share since you couldn't remember your side of it. I mean, what if I had been wrong?"

I purse my lips to keep from smiling.

That's sweet.

God, why is he so cute? How did I miss this side of him all these years?

"All right. Thank you. But also, you suck." I move into the apartment and sit on the couch where he'd been sitting. He takes his seat again and mutes the TV.

"What else did you learn? Maybe I'll know a piece of that, too."

I bark out a laugh. "Okay, so can you tell me why I haven't had sex in more than a year?"

His expression turns stony. "Was it that prick who owns those hotel chains that I kicked out of my bar?"

I gasp. "Hudson! I think so. Brooke said some rich asshole. It has to be one and the same."

Hudson chuckles.

I smack his arm. "Why did you kick him out?"

"Because he slept with you and was bragging about it."
I lean back to take him in.
He clears his throat quickly.
"So you defended me?"
He nods.
"Even though we did nothing but fight?"
"Fighting or not, Sadie, you deserve to be respected."
I smile so wide my cheeks hurt.
"What?" he groans.
"You've closet liked me all these years, haven't you?"
"No," he says quickly and unmutes the TV.
"Admit it. Yes."
He shakes his head again, but a small smile touches his lips.
"That's enough talking for tonight."
I open my mouth to say more, but then close it. Of all the comebacks I could have said, the one I want to say most takes me by surprise.
If he doesn't want me to talk anymore, maybe he could kiss me to shut me up.
Oh wow, I really do love enemies-to-lovers.
I let out a bubble of laughter at my own thoughts.
Hudson eyes me curiously.
If only he knew.

CHAPTER SIXTEEN

HUDSON

Tourist season is always good for the bar. It's busy from opening until closing, and I like being busy. I like not having time to dwell on the things I can't change. I'm fully aware of my obsession with things not turning out the way I thought they would. It's a great reminder of why I take things day by day.

Although this past week has been interesting, to say the least.

"How is your day going, Boss?" Betty asks as soon as I step behind the counter of the bar to help her with the lunch rush. I'm going to man the bar while she waits tables with Shelly.

"Good."

"It's just good? I feel like this past week has been overly eventful for you." She tilts her head to the corner.

The prime spot for sunlight, so I've been told recently.

The day after Sadie and I made lemon bars in the bakery, she came down here to the bar, moved a couple of chairs around, and put what she calls her reading chair right where the windows meet in the south and east corners of the building. She's got a little table next to it with flowers, and there's a second chair across from her in case someone wants to join her. I won't lie, when she isn't using it, people flock to it. I've always had a basic industrial-looking bar. Chairs, tables, longer high-top tables, and the bar top. But her little seating area has been a nice place for those who want to just enjoy a beer without taking up an entire table.

Adding more areas like that wouldn't be a bad idea. More comfortable chairs and possibly even a few couches. Fill the place with more homey vibes.

But I also love that Sadie's made herself at home here and in my apartment.

It's a feeling I never thought I'd have again. The ease of living with someone. Going home at night and knowing she's there makes me feel lighter. Relaxed. The last girlfriend I lived with was nice enough, but Sadie is one of a kind. She doesn't expect anything from me the moment I step through the door— she just enjoys being around me.

Which is mind-blowing.

Sadie's officially been crashing in my room for the last week. Every morning, she wakes up early and heads to the bakery. I didn't follow her today. At some point, everyone needs to give her space to be her again, and right now, as she holds a book in one hand while sipping her iced tea, I can't help but think the smile on her face means that she's starting to feel more like herself than she has in a while.

Hell, maybe even before the accident. The fact I'm noticing this is also astonishing.

Maybe it's the dinners we have cooked together or the fact that she's just as obsessed with *Wheel of Fortune* as I am. Hell, these are the most mundane things, but with her … it's better.

I blow out a breath as I turn my focus back to Betty.

"Things are good."

"Oh man," she says with a click of her tongue.

"What?"

"You like her. *Like her*, like her."

"I ..."

My answer stalls because the Sadie I've been hanging out with and the Sadie I grew up with are two different people. This one makes me feel something, yes, but I'm not an idiot. Her memory will come back, and it's in my best interest not to get attached to this version of her.

I choose to go with "It's just nice to see a different side of her."

"Okay. I won't press the topic."

Betty moves out from the bar to greet a new table, leaving me with my thoughts as I wipe down the counters.

Sadie and I haven't done much to help her memory since we made our little agreement. She's been doing her own thing, which, in my head, is just as important. So, I guess, in a way, I am helping by letting her lead. She's not stressed when she's just being her.

That's the best approach. One that isn't forced. Then again, maybe I should recommend a few ideas. Her brother and her dad have stopped by. She always seems irritated when Linc leaves, but the look she gives her dad is gentler.

I have no doubt that she cares for her brother, but he can be a bit overprotective. I know that they invited her home for dinner this weekend, but she didn't give them an answer yet. She's avoiding her own house because she's not ready to see how it moved on, and she didn't. That should be what I help her with next. I just need to find a way to do it.

"I think we need to go to Wind Valley," Sadie says, startling me and pulling up a seat at the bar with a sigh.

"And why is that?"

"The couch is still delayed. It's been almost a week. It's in Wind Valley. What if we just drove there and got it ourselves?"

It's not the worst idea, considering after a week of sleeping on my current couch—well, it needs to go.

I'd have to recruit my brothers to help me get it up the stairs, but that's easy enough.

"Okay, when?"

"Really?" She perks up "Can we go right now? I'll call them."

"I'm working."

"I've got this," Betty chimes in, appearing out of nowhere. "You two get that new couch together. I'm not so sure I can keep watching him hobble around on that leg."

I scowl at her.

For the last couple of days, anytime Sadie saw me limping, we argued over who was sleeping on the couch and who was sleeping in the bed. So far, I have always won. I've since decided to push through any pain when she's around so she won't notice. But it seems my bar manager is going to blow my cover.

"You told me it didn't hurt." Sadie folds her arms in front of her and glares at me.

"It doesn't."

Not right now anyway.

"Did you lie so that I would stop asking you to switch our sleeping spots?"

I sigh, loudly.

"You could have shared the bed," Betty says as if she's part of this conversation.

Sadie's hand goes up. "I offered, and he shut me down real fast on that one."

"I bet he did," Betty replies. Her mouth opens to say more, but I beat her to it.

"I just need to fuel up, and we can go."

I move quickly around the bar and nod for Sadie to follow.

She hops off the stool with a smile and her book. "I love road trips!"

———

TWO AND A HALF HOURS LATER, the couch is loaded and strapped down in the bed of my truck.

Sadie is already in the passenger seat and waiting for me by the time I come outside of the gas station.

I hop in and hand her a diet soda from the fountain and a small bag of white cheddar popcorn.

She pulls the bag open right away.

The entire trip to Wind Valley was spent with Sadie asking me question after question about our relationship before her fall. What do we fight most over? *Anything and everything.* Who wins most of the fights? *Me, naturally.* Why do I come to the bakery every morning if I don't like her? That one I laughed at and told her that you can be good at what you do and still have people not like you. Hence, why I kept showing up. Sadie just smiled at my answer and kept shooting off rapid-fire questions.

Anyway, it doesn't surprise me when I pull onto the road and she starts talking again.

"How did you know I'd like this combination of snacks?"

I shrug. "You always ask for these instead of chips at the bar."

"And the drink?"

"You either ask for diet or iced tea, and the store didn't have iced tea."

"Hmm. For someone who used to hate me, you sure know a lot about me."

Yeah, I do. I mean, part of my job is to remember those who come in frequently, but I couldn't tell you what chips Mr. and Mrs. Winter like to eat or drink.

"I would have thought that with our history, you'd pretend I wasn't there or choose not to wait on me. From what I gather, I'm picky, I'm bossy, I'm—"

"You are many things, Sadie, but invisible is not one of them."

This makes her pause. I sort of like that I made her speechless, even if it's short-lived.

"Still, I like that you know all these weird facts about me. But I feel like I don't know much about you. Not now that we are adults."

I nod. I don't really like to talk about myself, but from her view, right now, it must seem like everyone knows her better than she does, so maybe I can give her some peace and let her know something about me that most people don't know.

"What do you want to know?"

"Oh, so much." She smiles teasingly at me. "What are you willing to share?"

I think it over for a moment, then tap the lid on her drink. "I don't like pop. Water, flavored water, or beer is all I need."

She holds up her popcorn bag.

"I'd pick baked barbeque."

"Favorite shirt brand?" she asks.

"Is that a thing?"

"Is it for you?"

"No."

"Favorite shoes?"

"Tennis shoes."

"Colored socks?"

I chuckle. "Just white."

"White isn't a color."

I fake a gasp. "It is too a color."

"A boring one."

I'm about to ask her to ask me something else when she jerks forward in her seat.

"Oh! Is that an ice skating rink?" Sadie asks, her eyes wide as she grins and points out the front windshield. "We have to go."

It's the Wind Valley Recreation Center. I went there a lot as a kid. Since Lovers doesn't have a year-round ice rink, my parents put me in private lessons on the weekends. Once I made the team, it made for a lot of long days to practice during the week. They had to take me out of school early on those nights just so we could make it. Which meant they left work early and put in a lot of time to help my dream come true.

All for me to be in the wrong spot at the wrong time and let it all fall apart.

That was the last time I was on the ice. I didn't even try after the accident because I could barely walk. I wasn't stupid. I knew the doctors were right.

So yeah, my skates have been packed ever since that night.

"I don't think ice skating is something you should do," I tell Sadie. "If you slip and hit your head, that would not be good. Your father and brother would kill me, and you know it."

She rolls her eyes. "Oh, please, Hudson. If I go with you, I can hold your hand the entire time, and if I start to fall, you can catch me."

I let out what sounds like a grunt.

"Like I said, your brother would kill me if I let you do this."

And yet, my body steers the truck to the parking lot.

"It's a good thing I'm not asking for your permission then, isn't it?"

She pulls on the door handle to get out.

"Sadie, wait," I call out, doing the same. I rush behind her as she practically jogs to the front doors. Not only have I not been on the ice, but I also haven't been inside a rink since my accident.

Not one foot. Never even been this close to one.

My coach brought me all my personal belongings once the final decision was made, and I was released. He brought it to my house, and he stayed for maybe five minutes making awkward small talk. Maybe he had somewhere to be, or maybe the relationship I thought we'd built over the years was a joke. Either way, I never heard from him after that.

Sadie stops abruptly and turns on her toes. "Oh, are your skates in your truck?"

"What?" I ask.

Her question, although logical, throws me off.

"I'd assume you'd always have them with you for occasions like this, right?"

I shove my hands in the pockets of my jeans and drop my chin to my chest. I'd like to think there's a way for me to get out of this situation. Convince her that this a bad idea because of her head and what not, but let's be real: this is Sadie. Nothing I say —or anyone else says, for that matter—can stand in her way.

"I haven't been at a rink in a while." I'm still looking down at the cement sidewalk.

Silence floats between us, so I chance a look up.

She's looking at the rink now, her lips twisted as if she wants to say something but is trying to decide whether it's a good idea or not.

Suddenly, her gaze flashes to mine.

"Do you want to go inside?"

Fuck yes, I do.

But I spent the last three years putting this life behind me so I can move on. What's going to happen to me if I step in there? Will I get flashbacks? Will I get angry as the memory of everything I lost floods back to me?

"Let's just go home," Sadie says quickly and starts for the truck. "We can get the couch moved in, and then we can just—"

"Yes," I finally answer her before she can get too far away. "I want to go in."

"You do?"

Her golden gaze meets mine, and even though I'm hesitant to confirm my answer, the glow of her hair as the sun sets behind her reminds me of what she's been through since she showed up at my door.

She wants to be better. She wants to make sense of things. She wants to find herself again.

If I have even an ounce of her courage when it comes to the ice, I'll be okay.

"I'll go in if you go to your dad's this weekend for dinner."

She rolls her eyes. "That's a dirty trick."

I shrug.

"And … will you come with me—inside, I mean?"

She bites her bottom lip with a nod.

"Of course, I will. Since you'll be coming to dinner with me as well."

I should have seen that one coming.

I nod, and then we don't say anything else as we get to the doors. I freeze, and Sadie doesn't rush me. Instead, she just stands next to me for as long as I need.

It feels like hours, but in reality, it's only seconds before I feel her hand slide into mine, her fingers lacing with my own and curling to hold on tight.

I look to my left to see her watching me. She doesn't signal to the door or make any kind of gesture that I should make my move. She just stares right back at me. As if she knows this moment can't be rushed.

I feel like a wimp. I mean, hell, I'm a grown man. I should be able to walk in there and face my fear, but it's not that easy.

Her hand squeezes mine once more, and for some reason, the warmth of her next to me is all I need. Without letting go, I open the door and walk in, pulling her right behind me.

The smell hits me first, followed by the sound of the Zamboni cleaning the ice. This place looks exactly the same as I remember, but I don't have time to go down memory lane. The chatter from the locker room gets louder, and suddenly, boys who, by their size, I can only assume are in high school start to filter out.

The one at the front of the group stops in his tracks. He swings his helmet in one hand and holds his stick in the other.

"Dillon, slap me," he says and hits the back of his hand against the chest of his teammate next to him.

"Why?" the other kid asks.

"Because I'm 100 percent certain that *the* Hudson Asher is standing in our rink, looking right back at me."

I nod hello and wave with the hand that isn't locked with Sadie's. I could let go, but I don't want to, and neither does she it seems.

"Oh, it's him all right," the other kid says, and then the entire team rushes out, all of them stopping to do a double take.

Finally, after a few seconds, the one at the front moves his stick to the other hand and reaches out.

I do the same and shake it.

"This is crazy. What are you doing here?" he asks.

"Do you live here?" another asks.

"Is it weird to ask if you can sign my skates?" someone asks from the back, starting a domino effect of requests.

"If we get to ask for things, I want to know his net move. It's a classic!"

"No, the one when he skates backward and can still make a goal."

One by one, they either high-five me or shake my hand. Sadie tries to pull away, but I keep her close.

"I think I need to see the kind of moves this team has first," I say in a joking tone that reminds me of razzing with my old team.

"Oh, you're in for it," one kid says, and then they all start up with the questions again.

"Whoa, whoa, this doesn't look like warm-ups," a man says as he struts from the locker room. He stops short when he notices the team's silence, and then sees me.

"Well, this tracks then," he says and holds out his hand. "Coach Beacher."

I shake it. "Hudson Asher."

The team erupts again, and then Coach Beacher shoos them onto the ice.

"Figure skating is right after us, boys—let's not lose any time tonight."

The boys hustle onto the ice, but their coach stays back with me.

"This was a nice surprise, and if you'd like to stay for practice, we'd love to have you watch. If you're still here at the end, I might even cut it early for the boys to chat with you if you'd like."

"I would," I say without missing a beat.

"Good to hear." He disappears into the rink, leaving Sadie and I alone. I walk closer to the glass and then take a seat.

"Are we staying for a bit?" she asks.

"Do you mind?"

"Not even a little." She sits next to me.

Her eyes drift to the players on the ice, but mine drift to her.

Did I think that I'd return to the rink one day? Yes. Is it better than I could have ever expected because of the woman next to me? Double yes.

"You're not watching the players," she says, never taking her eyes off the ice.

"I know." My voice catches, and she turns to me.

A smile touches her lips, and in a moment when I think I'd be stressed or worried or I don't even know, all I can think about is how those lips would taste. How would they feel pressed against mine? How, after all these years, all the fights, the feuds, the bickering … I can honestly say that I never, ever want to go back to how things were between us.

This version of us is my favorite.

CHAPTER SEVENTEEN

SADIE

"Are you sure you want to do this?" Hudson asks as soon as we pull onto my dad's street.

I nod.

"Are you positive? Because I know I made you agree to do this, but if you change your mind, I'll support you."

"I'm positive. I might not be ready to move back into my old room, but I can't avoid this house forever. This is the right next move for me."

I keep my eyes out the front window, the row of houses that I grew up with passing by. At least the street looks the same.

Hudson doesn't say anything, so I turn to him.

"This is the right move, right?"

He shrugs. "I can't answer that for you, but if you feel it is, then yeah. This is all on your terms, Sadie. Don't let anyone rush you."

I nod again, because clearly that is the only response I have right now.

"It is."

Hudson pulls the truck to a stop in front of my dad's house.

The first thing I noticed when I came home from the hospital was the fresh coat of white paint and the new blue front door. Mom would have loved that blue door.

I bet he did that for her. I just wish I knew how he coped with everything. I hope my living with him for the last few years helped. I don't have to remember everything to know that it helped me. My life was on track somewhere, wasn't it?

I startle when Hudson appears at my door and opens it.

"Are you staying in the truck?" he asks.

"No, I was just looking at the house."

He twists to look too.

"Is it different?"

"Yes and no. The paint is fresh, and the door is a different color, but other than that, it's the same."

We walk up the driveway, and I spot the handprints in the cement Linc and I made as kids. I see the rock that has our address engraved on one side and our height markings on the other side.

I let out a breath and feel my shoulders relax.

It is my home. I just … I wish I remembered more, and I'm so tired of wishing for that.

I hear my dad's laughter the moment we walk inside, and we both follow it to the back of the house.

Dad and Linc are out on the patio, sitting at the table and drinking beer. There's a chips and dip spread, and I can smell the burgers cooking on the grill.

"Look at you two having a good time," I say, making our presence known.

They look up at the same time, and I swear, I've never seen my dad smile bigger.

"Sadie," he says and gets up, swiftly pulling me into a hug.

"Hi, Dad."

He pulls back, taking only a step and still holding my hands to look me over.

Then he turns to my brother. "See, Linc, she's doing great without us breathing down her neck."

Dad winks at me. "He's such a dad sometimes."

I laugh, and so does Hudson. Next thing I know, Dad and Hudson are doing a man hug and slapping each other on the back.

"You're not tired of her yet?" Dad asks.

Hudson grins as his gaze connects with mine. "Trust me, no one is as shocked as I am. She's almost to peaceful to be around."

I roll my eyes.

"Perhaps I'll have to strike up an argument later to keep you on your toes," I say and grab a beer out of the little cooler my dad brought outside.

"Perhaps I'll have to remind you that I almost always have the last word."

"Perhaps I'll—"

"Perhaps I'm going to vomit if you two keep this up." Linc grabs the beer from my hand before I can take a sip. He points between me and Hudson. "What is this right now? Are you two flirting?"

"Linc," I scold as Hudson smoothly takes my beer out of my brother's hand and hands it back to me.

"No," Hudson answers. "You're just not used to seeing us get along."

I smile before I take a sip. "Yeah, what he said."

Both Hudson and my brother gawk at me. One has amusement with a little of something I can't quite figure out yet, and one has a look that says *I'm about to whoop your butt like I did when we were kids.*

I laugh and spin to find my dad in the kitchen.

"Do you need help?" I ask.

He turns from slicing onions and tomatoes. His eyes fall to the beer in my hand.

"Oh, don't tell me you're going to take this away from me too."

He chuckles and shakes his head.

"Nope. You're a grown woman, Sadie—you can make your own choices."

He says it so calmly that the next question comes out of my mouth before I can't think twice about it.

"Is that why you haven't pestered me to move back home?"

He nods slowly. "Partly. On the one hand, I'd love nothing more than to be here with you each day while you recover, but on the other hand, I also know you well enough not to push you. Plus, Hudson's a good man. I trust that he's taking just as good of care of you as I or your brother would."

Yeah, he is. I wish he'd take a little better care of me in other areas, but that's probably not something to share with my dad.

"He is a good man." I let my gaze drift to where Hudson and Linc are by the garden. Linc is probably gushing over the tomato plants again. He does this every year, even before Mom passed, so I know I didn't miss anything in that area.

What I did miss was the way Hudson is standing. Such confidence. The way his entire body owns the space he's in. Not to mention the jeans he picked out today. They fall straight over his legs, but they hug his butt in just the right places. He reaches back to scratch his neck.

He has big hands, and those fingers would—

Dad clears his throat, and I nearly jump out of my own skin.

"Dad!" I place a hand over her heart. "What?"

"It's not polite to stare, Sadie."

"I wasn't staring."

"Mm-hmm. Just help me take this outside. Dinner is almost ready."

Soon enough, the four of us are all sitting at the table eating dinner, sharing stories of who snuck out better in high school. Then, of course, after story time, I crush all three of them in a friendly game of poker.

The loser has to do the dishes.

Linc's favorite.

"Are you sure you don't want to stay?" Dad asks as he hugs me goodbye.

I spot a picture of me and him on the mantel and sigh. I have no idea when that was taken.

"Not tonight."

He leaves it at that.

"Bye, Linc!" I shout toward the kitchen, where the water is running.

"Goodbye!" he yells back in a grumpy tone.

"See you soon, Mr. Collins." Hudson shakes my dad's hand.

Once we are out the front door and back in his truck, I relax into his seat. I was fine until I saw that picture. For a brief moment, I was so caught up in the night and the company that I forgot I'd forgotten so much.

"How do you feel?" Hudson asks as we pull onto the road. It'll be a quick drive, but I'm glad we drove instead of walking.

"Fine."

"Fine?" he repeats. "Fine, as in this is where you strike up an argument, or fine, as in it wasn't good and it wasn't bad?"

I let out a soft laugh.

"The latter."

"How do you feel about that?"

"You sound like a therapist," I tease. "Ask it the way it first comes to your mind."

He shakes his head. "No."

"Do it."

"No." Now he's laughing.

"Just ask me the question the way Hudson would ask it."

"No."

"Hudson!"

"Fine. On a scale of one to ten, how much do you want to cry right now?"

I open my mouth, ready with a smart-ass remark, but pause. That definitely wasn't what I was expecting.

I start to crack up, and then shove his arm.

"Wow."

"You said to just ask it."

"I know."

"That's why I think them through."

"You can't now. I know how your brain works."

He just shakes his head.

I think his question over for a moment.

"A three."

His brows shoot to his hairline. "A three, huh?"

I nod. "One for the picture I saw when I left, one for how Dad looks at me when they mention something I don't remember, and one for us."

"Us?"

"Yeah."

"How do you figure that?"

"Because it took me hitting my head a little too hard for us to become friends. It makes me sad."

He pulls into a spot behind the bar, gets out, and opens my door for me.

"Don't waste any tears on me, Sadie. I'm not worth it, and besides, after another week as my roommate, you'll be singing a different tune. One that will have you eager to not remember the past—you'll simply just want to move forward and be happy again."

We ascend the steps in silence as I think over his words.

Is that what he wants? I saw the way his face lit up at the rink. He misses that life, but there is a reason he hasn't been back. Is he still struggling to move forward and be happy, as he put it?

There are things I want to remember, yes, and remembering them would be nice, but ultimately, that's what I want too.

To just move on and be happy.

"Hudson." I reach for his arm as he opens the door.

He spins quickly, then lets go of the door and takes a step down toward me.

"What is it? Do you remember something?"

Is my expression alarming? I lock my gaze with his, and for a split second, I'm convinced that I see panic in his eyes.

"No," I say quickly and look away.

He lets out a breath. "What's going on then?"

"What you just said," I start. "I've been trying so hard to remember my life, yet nothing is coming back."

Hudson doesn't say anything as I pause to think how to say it.

"I still do, but if I keep obsessing over it, I might not ever move on. I don't doubt that I was happy with my life, career, and even the fact that I was living with my father. But I … I can't keep hoping for something that might not ever happen. I want what you just said, to move forward and be happy again."

"Good."

"I was hoping you'd do it with me."

"Sadie, I …"

A vision of him at the rink the other day consumes me once again. I know he understands what I'm feeling.

"We both deserve the future we want, right? Even if it's different from our original plans."

After a moment, he nods. "It's only been a couple of weeks, Sadie. Your memory still has a chance to come back."

"It might, but I'm done waiting for it. I want to *live* again, I want to be happier than ever before, and I think you should do that with me."

His eyes turn dark, and for a moment, I think I've crossed the line. He shared things with me at the ice rink that I believe he hasn't shared with his brothers. I want to help him the way he's helped me. I want to be there for him the way he's been there for me. I want—

"Okay," he says before my mind can get carried away. "Let's do it."

"Really?"

"Really." He smirks and then unlocks the door.

We both wander into the apartment, and as I head for the bedroom, he heads for the couch.

"Does this new move on and be happy approach in life mean you can suck it up and finally share the bed with m—"

"Nope."

I watch him peel his shirt off, revealing his sculpted back before he disappears into the bathroom and turns on the shower.

Move forward and be happy with Hudson.

I like the sound of that.

CHAPTER EIGHTEEN

HUDSON

I want what you just said, to move forward and be happy again.

I was hoping you'd do it with me.

Sadie's words have played over and over in my head like a broken record since she said them last night. Obviously, I've been living, but since the day she showed up and decided she was going to crash in my bedroom, things have been different. I'm not going to get all cliché and say that I wasn't living before her, but damn, I sure as shit didn't look forward to each morning the way I do now.

And that says more than I'm ready to admit.

"You should put me on the schedule."

I slowly raise my gaze from one of the sinks I'm filling before I open the bar to meet Sadie's eyes. She's rising from her window chair and walking toward me. The morning sun is at her back, giving her a glow that hits me right in the chest. This is becoming my favorite view of her.

She's beautiful.

"Schedule for what?" I ask, pulling my attention away from the way her entire face lights up as she smiles at me.

"To bartend."

I chuckle. "I know we missed a lot of years, but I'm pretty sure you've never been a bartender."

"No, not that I recall either, but you know, it's a little fuzzy in a few areas."

I cast a look her way. Her comment isn't funny, not to me anyway, but the way she's grinning at me makes it hard not to reciprocate the emotion.

"If you want to work, you can always go back to the bakery," I tell her. I don't really want her to go. I like looking up during the lunch shift to see her reading. I like having her close. Which is exactly why I won't argue with her if she chooses to go back to work.

"I don't want to go the bakery. I want to be here." She opens her arms wide. "There is just something about this space."

I'll admit, when I set out to open this place, I wanted it to be refreshing and bright and give people a sense of relaxation. The windows really help, and I can see why she wanted this place the way I did.

But it still stands that it might be time for Sadie and me to get a little space during the day.

I can't do anything with the attraction I feel toward her, so yeah, space is smart.

Instead of waiting for me to reply, she walks to the other side of the bar, hovers her hand over the bar top, and lets her fingers glide against it until she reaches the entrance. She steps through and grins at me.

I toss my towel over my shoulder, cross my arms, and lean my hip against the lower counter. Her hair is braided to the side, and she's wearing a white and purple sundress that's tied on the top of each shoulder. You'd think she'd pair it with some strappy sandals, but not Sadie—she's all about the white sneakers.

"What are you doing?" I ask when she gets so close that I swear she can hear the way my heart is pounding.

"Waiting for you to teach me how to bartend."

I glance at my watch. We don't open for another half hour. Everything is basically ready, and the things that aren't don't need to be prepared until right before the door is unlocked. I let out a sigh as she claps.

"I knew you'd cave for me."

I hitch a brow at her, and she rolls her eyes.

"Oh, stop, you knew it too."

Yeah, I fucking knew it, too, but I don't need her to know it. It's best if the two of us just keep on pretending that we don't feel a pull toward the other.

Denial.

It's been working this far. I need her to keep going along with it.

Especially after the ice rink.

Fuck. I don't know what it is about that night, but I cannot get her out of my mind. Having her there with me for a big moment like that felt right.

Too right.

She opens one of the glass coolers between us and pulls out a frosted pint glass. "Let's start here. I can pour a beer just fine from a can to a glass for anyone who loves extra foam."

I let out a howl of laughter. "So, what you're saying is, start from the very beginning?"

"Precisely."

I grab a glass just like hers and walk to the tap.

"Okay, so first, you'll start by pulling the tap back just slightly and keeping the glass a little sideways, like this," I say as I show her. "Let it pour into the glass slowly, and as you near the top, you'll steadily straighten the glass."

As soon as I'm finished, I hold a perfectly poured beer between us.

"Oh, that can't be too hard."

She steps in front of me to take her turn.

I know I should move back.

At least take one step.

Instead, I close my eyes and inhale the smell of her hair. It's lavender, a scent that should soothe me, but all it does it make my heart race even more and my blood turn hot.

I swallow, set the glass in my hand down, and clench my fists.

Don't touch her.

Don't do it.

A vision of me caging her between my arms and then pressing my lips to hers plays in my mind. What I wouldn't give to finally taste her. To hear the noises she makes when our bodies connect. To feel how soft her skin is against my fingers. God, going there with Sadie would be—

"Am I doing it right?" she asks, her sweet tone pulling me out of the tortuous daydream and into a reality that's equally teasing.

She spins quickly to show me, but I'm right in her space. I hadn't noticed how much I gravitated toward her while she was pouring something as mundane as a fucking beer.

My sudden movement to back up shocks her, so she backs up, too, but then hits her hip on the counter, and the glass in her hand slips to the floor and shatters next to her shoes.

"Oh shit. I'm sorry, Hudson," she says, bending quickly to clean it up.

My hand jerks between us quickly, my palm covering the corner before she hits her head on it.

She pauses, her forehead barely hitting my knuckles as her eyes focus on my hand.

My breathing increases. In a matter of seconds, she could have hit her head again, and it terrifies me. How quickly whatever this is between us could have just vanished.

Hell, I've smacked my head dozens of times, but Sadie can't risk that.

I won't risk it.

Sadie stands slowly, the broken glass forgotten.

I should say something, anything, but words can't express how I feel at this moment.

Electric and ready to combust.

My hand drops to her hip as I back her up to the bar top.

She gasps, her bottom lip dropping open as she sucks in her next breath.

I reach up, my thumb brushing her plump pink lips.

"These lips have been torturing me," I whisper.

Her eyes close, and her chest rises and lowers in quick pulses.

There is a list of reasons why I shouldn't kiss Sadie, and although they have been playing on repeat in my mind all morning long, right now, I don't give a damn about a single one of them.

Instead, I dip my head and press my lips to hers.

It's soft at first. As if this kiss is a question. Do we do this? Does this feel right?

She kisses me back, once, twice, and then she groans her answer.

I reach low, my palms gripping her butt as I lift her onto the counter and spread her legs to settle between them. On her next moan, I slide my tongue into her mouth and steal every ounce of air she might have.

The hands that lifted her up now thread through her hair, holding her in place as if she'll disappear if I let go.

Kissing Sadie is hypnotic. It's wild, it's passionate, it's as if I've finally figured out how to breathe life back into myself.

To be honest, I've felt myself living again the moment she showed up on my doorstep asking for a place to sleep, but this, this is on a whole new level.

Sadie Collins has changed my life in just a matter of weeks, and this kiss, this one kiss, is proof that life without her will never be the same.

And that thought terrifies me.

I break the kiss and take a step back, my hand covering my mouth as I control my breathing.

"I'm … I'm sorry," spills from my lips.

Whatever this is, it won't last once her memory comes back.

It's better that we just ... not.

"You're sorry?" she asks, and just when I think she's about to lay into me and give me a good tongue lashing like the old days, she smiles. "Fine. Be sorry. Just know that I'm not."

She jumps off the counter and readjusts her dress, now wrinkled at the sides. I must have bunched it up and not noticed because she had me so spellbound.

"Sadie, we both know that whatever that was isn't a good idea."

She finishes smoothing out her dress and lifts her head.

"Says who?"

"Me."

"Why?"

"Because."

She crosses her arms and cocks a hip, waiting for me to elaborate.

"Your brother would kill me," I tell her.

She nods slowly. "And your next excuse?"

I open my mouth, but nothing comes out.

She's right. Anything else that comes out will be an excuse.

I toss my hands up and let them drop my sides.

"Okay, then," she says and turns for the back room, looking over her shoulder. "When the checklist of why you think we can't do this runs out, come find me."

"Sadie …"

She stops and turns abruptly. "Don't Sadie me, Hudson. I've spent the last three years living a life I can't remember anymore. Maybe it wasn't one worth remembering. Maybe that's why I'm where I am now. I told you I'm done worrying about the choices I made before. I want to live in the present and move forward. Kissing you just now wasn't wrong. Nothing about it was wrong, and I plan to do it again, so I'm going upstairs now so that you can take whatever time you need to process the fact that no matter the obstacle life has thrown at you, you do actually deserve to take a risk again and you do deserve to be happy."

She doesn't even wait for me to reply. Not that I even know what I was going to say.

Is she right?

Is that what I'm doing, telling myself I can't have this because one part of my life was cut short? Do I think I'm not allowed to be happy again?

The door in the back slams, and I wince.

I turn back to the bar and spot the broken glass on the floor.

A month ago, I would have known what to do next. I'd have taken the safe route. The one in which I knew the results before it started. But right now, for the first time in a long time, I want to take the route that requires work.

I just … what if I put in the work and her memory comes back?

What happens then?

CHAPTER NINETEEN

SADIE

Men.

Arrgh.

I all but stomp the entire way up the stairs that lead to Hudson's apartment.

That kiss was the best kiss of my life, and he apologized for it.

Screw that.

I unlock the door and close it before dropping onto the couch.

I get it. He's best friends with my brother, and he doesn't want to do anything that would jeopardize their relationship, and yes, I understand that a month ago, we apparently hated each other. But that was then, and this is now, and oh my god, why can't it just be simple?

Girl meets boy, boy meets girl, they smile at each other, they ask to hang out, and then they kiss. Voila, they fall madly in love and live happily ever after.

It sounds so simple.

I grab a pillow off the couch and cover my face, letting out a scream.

I can't remember the last time I felt this way. Ever. I don't need to have memory loss to know this feeling, this *connection*, has never happened with anyone else.

I toss the pillow that muted my screams to the side and stand up.

I should go back down there. Communicate and tell him exactly how I feel. This is how it works, right?

Yes, this is how it works.

I jog down the steps and high-five Ian as I pass through the kitchen and march my happy ass back to the bar, ready to bare my heart to Hudson. But the moment I step out of the kitchen, I spot my brother sitting at the bar top. He's leaning forward on the counter, talking to Hudson, who is hunched over cleaning the broken glass.

"Sadie!" Smiling, Linc comes and hugs me.

I wrap my arms around him and squeeze him back.

"How are you today?"

"I'm good," I say with zero emotion and then look to the bar. My gaze instantly locks with Hudson's.

"I'm sorry. I should have cleaned that up before I walked out."

"It's fine."

"You broke the glass?" Linc asks. "Hud, you just said it was you."

Hudson sighs and goes back to cleaning.

"I forced him to teach me how to pour a beer, and then I dropped it, and then—"

"You walked out," Linc repeats my words.

I nod.

"Are you two fighting again?" he asks.

"No," Hudson answers quickly.

His tone in that one small word leaves me fighting a smile. He said it as if insinuating that we could ever disagree would be the worst thing to happen.

I like that he feels that way.

"Then why did you just walk out without cleaning?" Linc asks.

Silence fills the bar, but any response is forgotten when the doors open, and Betty's and Brooke's laughter steals our attention.

"I kid you not, three cups instead of one."

"You can't even fake that kind of mess up," Brooke says and then turns to us. "Hi, friends."

"Ladies," Linc says and returns to his barstool.

"Are we interrupting anything? We need to steal Sadie away for a bit," Brooke says. "Or, well, I do, since Betty is here for her shift."

"Nope. She's all yours," Lincs says. "Enjoy your day, sis."

The way he says it, all somber and sad, makes me want to hug him, so I toss my arms around him and squeeze tight.

He starts to laugh and then shrugs me off.

"Go!" He points at the door.

Brooke is still waiting for me, so I take my brother's advice and head for the door. Brooke loops her arm with mine and tugs me outside. As I look back, Hudson isn't even glancing in my direction.

Maybe he isn't as into me as I am him.

No, that's not it.

We're attracted to each other, and I feel like a fish out of water on what I'm supposed to do about it.

"I have a few things I want to run by you," Brooke says as she leads us to the bakery. "Do you know yet when you plan to come back?"

Forcing all thoughts of Hudson aside, I give her my full attention.

"No, I'm not sure yet."

"Do you want to come back?" she asks, and then she slaps a hand over her mouth.

"I'm sorry, that was …"

"A logical question and one I don't have an answer for. I really wish I did. I think it would help, maybe, I don't know. I'm a mess."

We step into the sugary wonderland, and I spot the glass display with all the baked goods Brooke has been preparing.

"Did you make all these?" I ask.

Her entire face lights up.

She nods. "Yes. The chocolate chip bar with coconut is new, but it's so good. Do you want to try one?"

"Yes!" I take a seat at one of the tables.

Brooke moves around the bakery with ease, a pleased smile on her face the entire time. She takes her time taking the dessert out and putting it on a plate. It seems like nothing, a job anyone could do, but it's not. Brooke woke up and wanted to be here. She wanted to bake. She wanted to make this specific treat, and the look on her face is nothing but pride.

She loves what she does.

I don't love this the way she does. I loved watching my mom here. I loved being a part of her world.

That's why I wanted to keep this place going. I wanted to be in her world for as long as I could.

The phone rings, so Brooke answers it. It's cordless, so she walks my plate to me, winking as she sets it down, and then disappears into the back.

I glance around the store as tears sting my eyes.

For the first time since I woke up in the hospital, I don't feel as if I just lost her. My heart misses her every single day, but I also know that she'd be sitting across from me, making me drink milk with the brownie and telling me that I need to follow my own dream and not hers.

I suck in a breath, fan my eyes, and bite into sugary perfection.

"I'm going to take that groan as your approval," Brooke says, walking back to the register.

"Oh, this is phenomenal. You should make these every week."

"Really? You think?"

"I think, yes."

She moves to sit across from me, and the smile on her lips fades. "Were you crying?"

I shake my head. "I was just thinking of my mom for a moment. I'm okay."

She studies me and then nods as if she accepts my answer.

"So, what did you want to talk to me about?" I ask and take another bite, one that is probably not ladylike.

It's just so damn good.

"Oh"—she waves a hand in front of her face—"it's nothing."

But her shoulders sag, so I know it's something more than she's letting on.

"You can tell me."

"I don't want to make you sad again."

"How could you do that?"

"Well, it's about the store."

"Oh. Are things not good?"

"No. Oh, no. Things are great. I just …"

"You just what?"

"I was thinking we should open an online store. From what you told me, your mom wasn't into that idea, but what if it was starter kits and other random things like boxes or trays or shirts with our logo and—"

"It's a great idea," I cut in. "Mom didn't like the idea only because she didn't want any food shipped to spoil, but if you can find a way, you should do it."

"We should do it," she corrects.

I nod, but when she beams with joy and starts talking about the online store again, a thought comes to me that I wish I'd noticed sooner.

Brooke should own the bakery.

Not me.

"Afternoon, ladies." Miles Asher walks into the bakery and stops. "Fuck, it smells good in here. What's that?" He points at my plate.

"A new treat Brooke made," I say, and I swear I see her cheeks turn a soft shade of pink.

"Do you have any more left?"

"Yes." She stands quickly. "How many do you want?"

"Just two for today," he answers and then takes her place across from me.

He's looking at me with a grin I've never seen before.

"How's your day going, Sadie? Good, I bet."

I cross my arms and lean back.

"Why do you have that same stupid smug look on your face that your brother gets when he knows something he shouldn't?"

He lets out a boisterous laugh. "Oh, we both know my brother well enough to read his facial expressions now, huh? Makes sense since I went to see him before the bar opened, only to see you sitting on the bar top with him—"

"I got it." But I fail miserably to hide my smile.

Brooke returns with the brownies, and he gives her his debit card as he stands.

"I just want you to know that I like this. Whatever it is between you two. I haven't seen him this happy in a long time."

He turns to look at Brooke, who is watching us now. "See you later, Brooke."

The moment he's out of the bakery, Brooke smacks the table.

"What is he talking about?"

I groan and cover my face.

"Hudson kissed me today."

"What!"

"Everything okay out here?" Daisy asks, and both Brooke and I nod.

Once she's gone, Brooke nudges my foot with hers.

"You didn't tell me?"

"It just happened. Right before the bar opened. I'm still processing it."

"Oh, please process faster. What does this mean?"

"Nothing, apparently. He said he was sorry and then started making excuses for why it can't happen again."

"Ugh. Typical."

"I know."

"What did you say?"

"I was very clear that I want it to happen again."

"Seriously? You?"

"What? I wouldn't do that with a guy?"

"I mean, not to Hudson. You hate letting him have the upper hand."

"I guess the old me would see it that way. The new me thinks I can't get enough of him."

Brooke squeals. "I love this for you."

"I'd love it more if he would just … let himself relax a little. I mean, it's not that I'm upset he won't do whatever with me, but it's like he thinks he can't be happy or have what he wants. He's so about following the rules and routine."

"I bet you could help him relax."

I let out a giggle and then toss a crumb at her. "It was a really good kiss. He propped me up on the counter and everything."

"And stood between your legs?"

"Brooke, he grabbed my knees and spread my legs to make room. It. Was. Sexy."

She squeals again.

"So now what?"

I shrug. "I don't know."

I should hate that I don't know what comes next. But then another customer comes in, and Brooke glows as they tell her their order.

Knowing what I'm going to do with bakery has taken a huge weight off my shoulders.

———

THE HALL LIGHT is still on by the time I return to the apartment later that night. After Brooke closed the bakery for the day, I went back to her place with her.

The more I thought about it, the more I obsessed over it, and the more I let myself grow a little embarrassed by what I said to Hudson.

Was I too blunt?

Did I sound desperate?

He was clearly letting me know that he didn't think anything between us would be a good idea, and here I was telling him that I didn't care what he thought because I planned to make it happen again.

I should apologize.

If the roles were reversed … well, let's just say I should respect his choice. If that's how he truly feels, I will be okay with that. Even if it sucks.

I get my key out, but of course, Hudson left the door unlocked for me.

The sound of the shower running is the first thing I hear when I step inside.

I let out a breath.

This gives me a few more minutes to gather myself.

He's going to think I've lost my mind, and maybe I can use that to my advantage.

No, no, I need to be honest.

I set my purse down on the coffee table and take my shoes off, placing them near the door right next to his.

Why do I love the fact that he lines his shoes up by the door instead of leaving them around the apartment? And I love my shoes next to his even more.

I close my eyes and turn.

You need to stop thinking of him this way.

If it's one-sided, that will leave you nothing but heartbreak.

But that kiss didn't feel one-sided.

Heck, he put his hand out to cover the corner of the counter so I didn't hit my head. It was a smooth move—and then he kissed me.

That means something. More than what he let on.

I head for the bedroom but startle when I'm passing the bathroom door and hear what sounds like all the bottles collapsing into the bathtub.

"Hudson?"

He doesn't reply.

"Hudson," I say again and lean my head to the door. "Are you okay?"

Suddenly, the door swings open, and there's a naked chest right in front of me. Beads of water run over his firm pecs and down his torso to the towel wrapped around his waist.

"You're home?"

I nod. "Yeah. I went to Brooke's for a while. I thought I would give you your space. Are you okay?" I point into the bathroom.

He nods. "I thought you weren't coming back."

"Oh. No. I'm here."

I'm looking into his eyes, but every now and then, my gaze slips to his body. I take a deep breath and step back before I do something I can't take back.

"I'm sorry for today," I tell him before I can lose my nerve. "It was wrong of me to tell you that I was going to kiss you again after you told me it wouldn't happen again."

He runs a hand through his wet hair. "Never apologize for speaking your mind, Sadie."

"Yeah, but you clearly didn't enjoy it, and I—"

"I enjoyed it."

"Oh."

I bite my lip and look up at him, unsure of what I should say next. His eyes turn steel blue as he steps toward me. I reach my hand out, and it connects with his bare chest.

His hands settle on my waist. One of them slides around to my backside as he grips my butt and pulls me against him.

His forehead rests on mine as he inhales.

I close my eyes and pray he can't feel my heart racing.

I wait for … what? I'm not sure.

But then I open my eyes to see him step back.

"It's late. You should go to bed," he says. "I just need to grab some shorts."

He moves into the bedroom, grabs his shorts, and walks right past me, who is frozen in the hallway.

"Goodnight, Sadie."

He closes himself in the bathroom to change, and I'm just about to demand he explain what the hell that was when I stop myself.

He wants a fight.

He wants me to get worked up.

It'll be easier for him that way. Easier for him to avoid this.

Well, too bad, Hudson Asher. If I don't get what I want, neither do you.

CHAPTER TWENTY

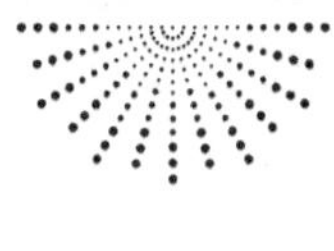

HUDSON

Work sucked again today.

All I thought about was Sadie and that kiss. It's been two days, and I can't even walk by that spot behind the bar without picturing her sitting there.

It's why as soon as Betty didn't need me anymore, I came upstairs for a cold, *cold* shower.

Lucky for me, Sadie had been out all afternoon, so I got a few more minutes to clear my mind of the day before she came home.

I thought if we started to argue again, my pull to her would fade, but she doesn't want to fight. No matter what I say or do, she doesn't argue with me.

She knows me better than I thought she did.

Which makes her even more perfect for me.

Shit.

I step out of the shower just as my phone begins to ring. I rub my towel over my scalp quickly to dry my hair, and then I wrap it around my waist.

"Hello?" I answer the unknown number.

"Is this Hudson Asher?"

I can't quite place the familiar voice.

"Yeah. Who's asking?"

"This is Coach Beacher, from The Rockets hockey team in Wind Valley."

Our first and only meeting flashes in my mind. The way I hesitated to go in and how Sadie grabbed my hand until we stepped through the door. Beacher had been right there when we stepped in. He hadn't given me time to panic; he was just as excited as the team to see me.

It was the reminder I needed to be aware that, just because the game ended for me, my memory and what I brought to the sport didn't.

Still, I don't recall giving him my cell phone number.

"Coach," I say, the greeting even more familiar than his voice. "What can I do for you?"

He chuckles.

"Right to the point, huh?"

"Well, I won't lie, I'm not sure what you could need from me."

"I hope it's okay that your girlfriend gave me your number before the two of you left the other day."

My girlfriend.

I don't correct him.

I should, but I don't.

I like the sound of it.

I shouldn't, but I do.

"It's perfectly fine."

"Good. Good. Listen, the boys really enjoyed your drop-in, and I was curious if you'd be interested in coming down for tomorrow's practice and teaching the boys a few things I don't know. I'm aware that it's last minute, and I apologize for not calling sooner."

I move out to the kitchen and grab a glass, filling it with water from the fridge.

Me, coach?

The idea of being back on the ice again, even for a day, sends an uneasy feeling to my gut. Yeah, I did it with Sadie, but that wasn't even on the actual ice and was mostly so that I didn't look like a fool in front of her, *and* to get her to go to her dad's house. Hell, she wakes up every single day and pushes through, but not me. I've been dwelling on my past for so fucking long, I'm not sure how to live life any other way at this point.

"Hudson? Are you still there?"

"I'm here," I tell him.

"I'll text you more details, and if it works out with your schedule, great. If not, maybe we can find another time to make it work."

"Of course. That sounds great."

"Thank you. The boys will be happy to hear it. I swear, they practiced harder than I've ever seen them after you spoke with them. You are a true inspiration."

"Thank you, Coach," I say but instantly feel guilty that I'm not as excited as he is or as those boys apparently are.

"Talk to you soon," he says and hangs up.

I'm still standing in the kitchen, reading the text Beacher just sent with more information, when Sadie walks in.

"I bought all the goodies to make chicken fajitas tonight, so I hope you're ready to get your—"

Her eyes widen, and she's biting her bottom lip.

"Are you okay?" I ask.

God, now that I know what that lip tastes like, it's all I crave. I almost slipped that night, too, but I forced myself to back off.

I'm not sure how much longer I'm going to last if she keeps looking at me like that, though.

She nods.

"O-kay." I step toward her, and she backs up.

She holds the grocery bags in front of her as if they are a shield at the same time I hold up my phone. "I just got off the phone with Wind Valley's hockey coach."

"Oh." She sets the groceries down on the counter and snaps her fingers. "I hope it's okay that I gave him your number. I meant to tell you after I did it."

"It's fine."

"Good. What did he want?"

"He wants me to come coach tomorrow."

"Seriously?" She claps. "That's great news."

I nod.

"Are you not going to do it?"

I shrug and then scratch the back of my neck. "I want to do it."

"Are you still nervous?"

"I haven't skated since that day," I admit. "I just—"

"What if I went with you?"

"I can't have you with me every time, Sadie."

"No, but I want to go. At least this time."

"Maybe," I say, although I'll tell her yes later. I don't want to be too eager.

"Look, I know this is your apartment and you can do anything you want, but do you want to go put some clothes on?" she asks, changing the subject quickly.

I glance down at my attire and chuckle. I'm still wearing nothing but a towel. Now her flushed neck and cheeks after she walked in make sense.

I smile over my effect on her for a brief moment, until my impact on her actually kicks in and makes my brain spin.

We kissed once, and yet it seems as though anytime we're near one another, every sense is heightened. I know the moment she walks into the living room by the way the hair on my arms stands up. I know she's walking toward me from the way her lavender scent gets stronger. I know the moment she wakes up because the sound of her bare feet against my hardwood floors is like a song.

A fucking song.

I'm so gone for this woman. It's insane.

But I'm the one who keeps saying we can't, so I need to be the one who pretends this situation is no big deal.

"How is this towel different from when I walk around in just my shorts or sweats?"

"It just is."

"I don't think it is, so how about you let me put the food away, and we cook dinner."

"Without you getting dressed?"

"I am dressed."

She stares at me for a moment as if she's deciding how much she should argue. This might be the subject that finally makes her crack. But she sighs and nods.

"You're right. Let me just go wash my hands."

"Thank you," I say, even though I want to gloat a little about the part where she said I was right.

She brushes past me to the bathroom. I hear the sink running as I put the food away, only keeping out what we need.

I'm just cutting open the chicken when Sadie emerges from the bathroom. I nearly slice my thumb off.

She smirks at me, wearing nothing but *her* towel.

Clearly, I underestimated her surrender a moment ago.

I set the knife down and cross my arms, leaning my hip onto the counter.

"What are you doing?"

She shrugs and saunters into the kitchen.

"I just thought I'd put on something a little more relaxed for the night."

"And you picked a towel?"

"Mm-hmm."

She grabs a cutting board and takes over, prepping dinner.

My gaze drops to her bare feet and slowly moves up to her lean calves and her thighs. The towel barely covers her round cheeks, so when she presses to the tips of her toes to get some seasoning from the cabinet over her head, a strangled noise hits me, and my cock hardens instantaneously.

I'm not so sure she kept her panties on.

"You're playing with fire, Sadie."

"Me?" She spins with her hand to her heart. "I'm not the one who refused to change his clothes. If you ask me, it's like you were asking for this."

"And what is this?"

Slowly, she moves toward me.

"For a reason that we could just innocently find ourselves half naked around the other."

I don't reply. I simply keep watching her.

There is not one single innocent thing about the way her gaze hardens as she looks at me or the way her tongue swipes over her lips with each step, or about the thoughts in my head.

"I think I made myself clear on where I stand," I repeat.

Hold strong, man. You can do this!

"And I think you're full of shit."

"Sadie," I say with as much warning as I can. I should know by now that the only person who knows me better than I know myself is her.

Fighting or not, we have a connection that can't be matched by anyone else.

"I'll give you one chance, Hudson. I'm right here, telling you that you can do anything you want to me."

Fuck.

"I won't beg, not unless you ask me to, but you should know that I'm not wearing any panties under th—"

I move so fast that her breath hitches. I spin us around and grip her hips to prop her on the counter. Then I spread her legs just like I did the other day and step between them. She moans when I press myself flush to her body, and I can feel her heart race as I lean my forehead to her chest.

Just once.

One time only.

It doesn't even have to be sex, but I have to touch her, taste her, and hear the way she sounds when she falls apart.

I need to consume her more than I need air to breathe.

Her fingers thread through my hair and tug just hard enough for me to lift my head and look her in the eyes right before I kiss her. I hold the back of her head as I slip my tongue into her mouth and kiss her hard.

Then I kiss from her jaw to her neck, to her chest.

"I think it's been too long since we both got what we wanted, Hudson."

I growl. She's right, but I refuse to take my mouth away from her to reply.

"Yes," she says and then lifts her ass off the counter to rub against my erection. My hands fall to either side of her, and I force her to sit back down, only to drag her to the edge.

She moans even louder when I push her towel higher onto her hips so she can feel more of me.

"Is this what you want?" I press my lips to her neck again as I grind my body to hers.

She nods.

"I need to hear you say it."

"Yes."

"Or is this what you want?" I slip one hand between her thighs and run my fingers up her skin until I reach her pussy.

"Fuck, Sadie, is this how I make you feel? Do you get this wet just thinking of me?"

"Yes," she breathes. "Every time I'm around you, my body craves you."

I slide two fingers inside her slowly and capture her lips with mine on her next gasp. My tongue slips into her mouth as I curl my fingers.

Her hips buck against me, and I smile.

"You're responsive. I like that."

I start to move my fingers in a circle, my thumb pressing against her core.

"Yes," she moans louder. "Keep doing that."

Her head falls back, so I take this time to keep kissing her neck, her collarbone, and her chest again. The hand that isn't working to bring her joy grabs the towel, pulls the knot apart, and tosses it to the floor.

The most perfectly round and perky pair of breasts bounce in front of me as she rides my hand.

The urge to feel them takes over. I remove my hand and pull her even closer to where her butt is hanging off the edge. I drop to my knees and just as she starts to argue, I take one long slow lick against her.

Her thighs are resting on my shoulders, but the moment I suck her clit and reach up to grip her breasts, her legs clamp against my head.

"Hudson!" she screams out. "Holy shit!"

I look up just in time to see her brace her body with one hand behind her and then move the other to thread through my hair. The fire in her eyes as she watches me eat her pussy like a fucking snack I've been waiting my whole life for only fuels me.

I love the full feeling of her tits in my hand, but I want to see her fall apart more.

I pull one hand away and press my fingers back inside as I

keep licking. Faster and faster. When I feel her walls clamping down on me, I pull my fingers out, twist my head, and lick as far inside of her as I can. Her hand on the back of my head holds me in place tighter, practically pressing my face in between her legs.

"Ahh! I'm coming, I'm coming, I'm coming."

I don't let up until the most beautiful sigh comes from her lips.

"Oh my god," she says quietly as I slowly stand. She's still splayed out for me on the counter, naked, her knees wide. I can see her pulsing between her legs, and that view alone has me grinning before I look her in the eye.

"Better?" I ask and raise a brow.

She starts to laugh, and the sounds hit me in the chest. I told myself just once, but feeling her, hearing her, and now seeing her after she comes—once won't be enough for me.

"Can I have my towel back?" she asks, pressing one foot against my chest and forcing me to step back.

I bend down to get it as she hops off the counter.

"Arms up," I say, and she does as she's told. I wrap the towel around her and knot it at the top. She drops her arms as if I'm done, but I pull her to me and gently press my lips to hers.

While I intend for it to be a soft kiss to conclude what just happened, Sadie has other plans. Her hand moves to my waist and grabs the towel, but I wrap a hand around her wrist and stop her.

She breaks our kiss and looks at me.

"Is this the moment where you say no, no, Sadie, tonight was about you and not me?"

I chuckle at the deep voice she uses to imitate me.

"It is, isn't it?" she asks and rolls her eyes.

"No, this is the moment I tell you that if you touch me, I'll have no choice but to strip you naked again, put you on this counter, *again*, and fuck you so hard that every tenant on this block will hear you scream my name."

Her bottom lip drops as she sucks in a breath. "Is that supposed to scare me?"

Again, I chuckle.

This woman will be the death of me.

I've already crossed a line by putting my face between her legs.

I hold her arms at her sides and step back.

"I'm going to go take a cold shower,'" I say and move around her. "Again."

She laughs. "Better lock the door."

I refuse to look back as I drop my chin to my chest.

The woman of my dreams, ladies and gentlemen, who also happens to be my best friend's little sister and who has forgotten how much she hates me.

Her laughter grows deeper, and I finally spin to face her.

"Sadie."

"Yes?"

"For the record, every night should always be about you."

For once, she doesn't have anything to say.

She bites her lips and nods.

And then I proceed to take the coldest fucking shower of my life.

I might not know a lot of things, but one thing is for sure; I have a choice to make.

End this now or chance losing the most amazing woman I've ever met.

CHAPTER TWENTY-ONE

SADIE

I should have brought a heavier coat.

A shiver runs up my spine as I rub my hands together.

I've never been a big sports kind of girl. Growing up, I thought I wanted to be. It was the typical scenario where, maybe if I knew football, I could talk stats with our school quarterback, and then he'd notice me. Or maybe if I knew baseball, the pitcher on our town's team would ask me out. Or even if I could dribble a basketball between my legs in one smooth motion, the point guard would take me to prom.

I learned just enough to know one position on each team. Heck, at the time, it was the position that mattered to me because of who was playing it.

Still, as I hear skates glide on the ice right now and sticks fighting for the puck, hockey was the one sport I intentionally took zero interest in. The obvious reason I didn't care about it is currently standing in front of a team of boys, and one by one, they're showing him the move he just taught them. I will be honest; I have no idea what it's called. Even after all the times I watched his games without anyone knowing, I didn't really pick up on the terminology. I was too dazed by the way he moved and how the fans loved him to learn anything else.

Should I want to know more? Maybe a little for Hudson's sake, but honestly, I love that we have found other things to bond over. I don't feel the need to impress him. I feel more myself with him than anyone else, and just thinking about it makes my heart beat a little faster.

No, what makes my heart race is thinking of last night.

The way he kissed me.

The way he touched me.

Hell, the way he *licked* me.

I know starting something between us is complicated, and I'm trying to let him sort it out on his own by not bringing it up, but god, the memory of how he made me feel is heavy, and I want more of that with him.

Only him.

Maybe I should give him space, but I don't want miscommunication to be our downfall. Tonight, I'm telling him that I'm all in.

I blow out a breath into my hands.

Gloves. I will bring gloves next time.

Of course, there is a door that would lead me to warmth and concessions if I wanted, but it's not the same out there.

I said I wasn't into sports or hockey, but I'm aware enough to know that watching this team would not have the same effect if I weren't in this section where the action is happening.

Coach Beacher blows his whistle, and quickly, the boys all get into some kind of formation. Hudson grabs the helmet the coach offers him and then glides to his own spot.

He's skating.

Until this moment, they have just been running drills, but it seems they're putting the things they've been learning into action, and Hudson is going to do it with them.

I move to the edge of my seat as if that is going to change my view. Aside from me and a few other parents, there isn't anyone here. I'm sitting in the first row.

The whistle blows again, and all the players move into motion, but my eyes remain glued to one in particular. The one who, until today, hasn't been on the ice in three years.

My eyes start to blur, so I look up for a brief moment and blink until the tears vanish.

When I look back to the ice, Hudson is way ahead of the others, and he has control of the puck. His stick goes side to side, and I swear to god I know he's skating, but he moves so effortlessly that he appears to be floating over the ice. One of the players gains on him, but Hudson turns in a fancy circle, hikes his stick back, and hits the puck into the net.

"Yes!" I jump up, screaming and clapping. "Yes!"

Every player turns to look at me. That's when I remember that it's just a practice and not a game, but screw that. Hudson is flawless, and I love every minute of it.

I slowly sit back down, quietly celebrating, when I spot Hudson looking at me as he skates toward the coach on the other side of the rink.

He reaches the box thing and pulls his helmet off. The biggest smile I've ever seen on him takes over as his eyes lock on mine. For a moment, we just stare at each other.

Then he winks.

Oh lord. I am so totally screwed.

The team wraps up practice, so I hop up hastily and practically run to the warmth as soon as Hudson is off the ice and following the others toward the locker room.

A rush of hot air hits me, and I shiver.

Whoever thought of inventing a sport and making it extra cold needs help.

Well, maybe not much help, because seeing him score that goal as if he didn't need to try was sexy as hell.

I blow out a breath and then take my time soaking in the banners on the walls and the trophy case just inside the main doors. It seems like Wind Valley's hockey team is the best in the state of Wyoming. They have an insane number of trophies, and the pictures from the past years show how far they've come. Since each team photo is in a frame that has the year printed on it, I find the year my brother and Hudson graduated. I spot Hudson immediately. The smile he's wearing is very similar to the one he wore just moments ago.

I wish he'd smile like that more often.

It's clear that hockey is a part of him. I hate that I can't give it back to him. That I can't fix his injury and get his career back for him.

"We won state that year," Hudson says behind me, and I startle a little as I turn, stepping back so that we can stand next to each other. "It was the first time I'd pulled off a hat trick. I came close dozens of times, but I just never could get that third goal in a game. That day was wild."

When he was here the other week, he seemed timid to be here, but today is different. The air around him is lighter, brighter.

"In all the years you played, how many hat tricks have you pulled off?"

"Eleven," he answers without missing a beat. "I scored my last one just a few seconds before everything ... changed."

Slowly, he turns to look at me.

"Thank you, Sadie."

"For what?"

"For forcing me to walk in here the other week. For coming today. For reminding me that my life didn't end with my career; it simply just changed."

I swallow the lump in my throat and nod.

I will not cry.

I will not cry.

I will not cry.

"You're welcome."

I don't want to risk sounding too cliché, but while I stand here wishing he'd let me kiss him again, I swear he's wishing that he could let me. I swear he's standing here thinking about how much his life has changed and that, for once, it's not bad. That he can finally see that happiness is still out there.

He breaks the trance first, his hand touching the small of my back as he guides me to the doors.

"Also, I had no idea you had a fondness for hockey. You were very enthusiastic in there."

I huff out a weird noise. "It was easy to do while watching you. I liked it."

"Oh, was it now?"

"Mm-hmm."

He opens my door, and I climb into his truck. I reach for the handle so that I can close it, but he stops me.

"I guess that's just one more thing we have in common." He reaches into the truck, his hand cupping the side of my face. "I like watching you too."

I bite my lip. Although my body is internally doing the happy dance because I love everything he just said, the urge to crack a stalker joke is strong.

He must sense my thoughts because he laughs, backs up, and closes the door.

I think it's time to face reality.

I'm crazy about Hudson Asher, and there is no going back.

———

"WE SHOULD STOP to get burgers before we go home," I say as we pull into Lovers a little before six in the evening.

Even as I say it, it hits me how, despite our past and despite the feelings that are sitting as a steady ember between us, Hudson and I have created this life together in the past few weeks. I didn't know what to expect that day I showed up at his door and asked for his help, but it wasn't this. It wasn't waking up excited to see the way he's sprawled on the couch with a blanket half draped over his lower body, or cooking dinner in the evenings knowing he will be there and I'm not eating alone, or picking out water drink flavors at the store based on what he would like—and it sure wasn't driving home from an afternoon of watching him coach a group of high school kids and planning what we are going to grab for dinner and spend a night in, just the two of us.

I grin, but then look out the passenger window of his truck and try to hide my smile with my fingers.

I'm almost embarrassed at how giddy this man makes me feel. I mean, I've been excited to be in relationships before, but none of them have ever felt like this. I'm always on edge, in a good way, waiting for the next thing to happen. I can't wait to see him when we are apart, and when we are together, I'm always thinking of ways to make that time last longer. Which is absolutely silly, considering we're currently living together. And we aren't even actually dating. We're two people who have kissed a couple of times and who have done some extra sexy things in his apartment.

Fuck, it was hot.

"I actually had another idea for dinner," Hudson's smooth voice fills the truck.

I twist to face him and let my hand drop to my lap.

"What did you have in mind?"

"Well"—he clears his throat—"I knew today was going to be

… a day. I also knew that I wouldn't have even put a day like this in my path if it hadn't been for you, so I wanted a way to say thank you."

"O-kay." I glance out the front window as he pulls into his normal spot behind the bar. "A burger would have been fine. I don't need anything crazy."

"Ohhhh," he draws out the word, "but you deserve so much more than a burger." He nods to the building. "Come on. Let's go inside."

I'm opening the door and jumping out before he can reach my side. There's no hiding the smile on my face.

I'm not usually a surprise kind of person, but with Hudson, I can't wait to see what he has planned for me.

Oh god, what if he kisses me again? Or what if he plans to do more?

Did I shave today? Shit. I knew we were going to the rink when I got ready this morning, so I didn't really plan on wearing anything but layers.

The warmth of his fingers as he laces them through mine is like a beacon to the pit of my stomach. I've been around him dozens of times, but right now feels ten times more thrilling.

Just when I think he's going to open the door for the stairs that lead to his apartment, he opens the door to the bar's kitchen.

Eating at the bar? That's his surprise?

I really need to teach this man how it's done.

I'll have time.

The first thing I notice when we get inside is that there are zero people in the kitchen.

"Where is everyone?" I ask.

"I'm not sure."

I glance up at the door that leads to the bar and notice that the little glass square that gives you a view of the room is dark.

"Are you closed?"

"I'm not sure."

I stop and jerk him back to stop with me. This is his bar. There is no way he doesn't know what's happening.

"What are you doing?" I ask.

Instead of answering, he just chuckles.

"Trust me on this."

That's all he says. One simple sentence that speaks volumes. I know he's up to something and he knows I know, but instead of arguing, he just wants me to trust him.

The crazy thing is, I trust him with my entire heart.

I nod. "Okay."

It happens again. That moment where we just stand staring at each other. A perfect kiss moment. Our day has been full of them.

What the hell is this man waiting for?

Of course, he's the one to break the spell once again. He turns to push the door open, dropping my hand and stepping back for me to go first.

Instead of pausing to demand he tell me why he won't just kiss me when I know he wants to, I let his hand settle on the small of my back as we step through the door.

"Hudson?" I whisper after we step into darkness. There is a little light from the front windows, but someone has pulled all the shades to create a blackout on the inside.

"Surprise!" various voices cheer as the lights flicker on. The entire room comes into view filled with my friends, family, and a few other Lovers locals.

Brooke claps and jumps as she grins at me, and my dad holds up a glass I assume has some kind of ale inside.

"Happy birthday," Hudson leans down to whisper in my ear. "I know it's not till next weekend, but I had an opening that meant you were gone most of the day, so I took it." The warmth of his breath skirts around my neck and sends goosebumps all over my body. The sensation of him being so close hits me right between the legs, and although I am over the moon with joy right now, I would kill to turn around and pull this man back through that empty kitchen and up to his apartment, where we can be alone.

"It's about time you two got here," Linc says, sauntering toward us with two beers. He hands one to Hudson and one to me. "Don't overdo it."

I roll my eyes but don't have a chance to argue before Hudson playfully shoves his shoulder.

"Back off the birthday girl, all right. It's her night to do whatever she pleases."

"Yeah, but—"

"No," Hudson says in return for my brother's pathetic rejection. "It's. Her. Night."

Technically, my birthday isn't until next week, but I'll take this.

Linc narrows his gaze at the man behind me, but I love having someone in my corner for once. Hudson has been there since my accident, and it doesn't look like he's going anywhere anytime soon.

"Oh my gosh, can we tell her what's happening now?" Brooke asks, interrupting whatever my brother is trying to convey to Hudson with just a look.

"Yes, please. I swear I've been looking forward to this moment since Hudson brought it up last week, and the fact he moved it up a week is even better," Betty says.

Last week?

I glance back to gauge his reaction to her comment, but he's talking to his brothers. They seem to be teasing him about something. It must not be anything serious though, because they're all laughing.

Still, he planned this before he knew what today was going to be like. He planned it before he kissed me ... before last night.

Brooke grabs my hand, stealing me from my thoughts, and pulls me to the back right corner of the room.

I spy white balloons and two gold ones that read twenty-eight. There is a unicorn piñata hanging just behind them.

"On your twenty-eighth birthday," Brooke starts, "you thought it would be hilarious to get a piñata and fill it with candy like when we were kids. Of course, we only picked Reese's and Kit Kats, but still. In this corner for the next hour, we will celebrate you turning twenty-eight."

"And when that hour is up," Betty chimes in, "we will move to that front corner."

I glance to where she points to see big gold numbers that read twenty-nine. "We had a wing eating contest that year." Linc laughs. "You won, but I'm ready for a rematch."

I laugh, trying to keep the tears on lockdown.

"And after that hour," my dad says and locks his arm with mine. He turns me to face where Hudson is standing next to the gold number balloons that read thirty. They are held down by a balloon weight that sits on the little white and gold table between the reading chairs I added a few weeks ago.

My dad lets me go as Hudson approaches.

"When you are done with those birthdays, we will celebrate this one."

I bite my lip and then cross my arms, eyeing him curiously.

"You planned all this?"

He nods. "Thirty is a big year, but so were the last three years, so it's only right that you get to celebrate them."

I can't believe he did all this.

"I don't see my twenty-seventh birthday," I tease.

He rubs the back of his neck and moves past me for the bar. "Your dad and brother said you refused to celebrate that year since it was soon after your mom passed, so ..." He reaches for something behind the bar.

Suddenly, a gold two and a gold seven balloon appear.

"So, I wasn't sure where to put these."

I take a quick glance around the room. No one is really paying attention to us, so I take this moment to throw my arms around him and hug him as tightly as I possibly can.

He hugs me back, and after everything that has happened in my life, I've never felt more at home than right now.

I haven't just formed a crush on Hudson Asher.

I'm well on my way to falling in love with him.

CHAPTER TWENTY-TWO

HUDSON

I can't remember the last time I laughed the way I have tonight.

Year twenty-eight was a success. Sadie crushed that unicorn piñata, but if you ask Linc, he set it up for her. If you ask me, it's a good thing Linc didn't play baseball.

Year twenty-nine was underestimated. When Linc and Brooke told me about the wing-eating contest Sadie had on that birthday, I remembered them telling me back then how she ate more wings than Linc, and he claimed she cheated. Back then, I can admit that I agreed with him. But now, knowing Sadie and witnessing it for myself, Linc lost fair and square. To be honest, so did I. I might have put up a better fight if I wanted, but I was too busy watching her.

I wasn't lying when I told her that outside the rink. Watching her and being in her presence has been my favorite part of the past few weeks.

I'm well aware of the sap I've turned into when it comes to her, but I don't really care.

I didn't think there was anything left in this life for me to look forward to, for me to celebrate, but Sadie has proved me wrong.

I won't tell her this, not yet anyway, but it seems that after all those years of fighting, she might have been right more times than I care to admit.

As soon as the wings were gone and more pictures were taken, we all moved on to year thirty. It was much more laid-back, and everyone here has basically found a spot near the windows and her favorite chairs or around the bar.

I pour myself another drink and glance around until I find Sadie sitting by herself. She's watching the room, and as if she can sense my eyes on her, she smirks in my direction. I grab my drink and make my way toward her, taking the seat next to her. I'm close enough that our shoulders bump when either of us moves, and our thighs are flush against each other.

"Having a good night?" I ask.

She nods. "Are you?"

I smile. "It's one of the best."

"Is it because of the fact you were on the ice earlier or because all our favorite people are in this room right now?"

All our favorite people.

She's not wrong. Even through all the fighting, we shared a large list of important people in our lives.

"Both." I take a drink.

"Come on, admit it. You're happier tonight because just hours ago, you were on the ice and skating with all those—"

"You were on the ice today?" Luca comes up quickly.

"Skating?" Dad adds right behind him.

"Oh—" Sadie leans close to me and whispers, "Was that a secret?"

I shake my head. I can tell from her tone that she hoped I wasn't trying to keep it a secret.

I reach behind us and rub her back. "No, it wasn't a secret. I just didn't tell anyone about it because I wasn't sure how it would go, and I didn't want anyone to get their hopes up."

My father grins. "How did it go?"

"He was amazing," Sadie cuts in and then bites her lip as she lowers her chin to her chest, likely embarrassed for the outburst.

For me, my heart swells at the pride she clearly has for me.

"It was better than I expected."

"And you were with him?" Luca directs his question to Sadie, who simply nods.

"It was actually Sadie who put the whole thing in motion."

"It was not," she argues. "You said yes on your own."

"Well, I wouldn't have had a yes to answer with if you hadn't wanted to go inside the rink last week, and you're the one who gave the coach my number after the boys spotted me."

"How could I not? You should have seen your face. I'm not sure who was more excited, you or that team."

"Hey, I was shocked at how many of them knew who I was."

Sadie rolls her eyes and smiles. "You left quite the impression."

"Did I now?"

Before she has a chance to answer, a throat clears in front of us. We both snap our attention to my father, who is shaking his head and grinning. My brothers, now that Miles has joined us, both have similar looks on their faces. I'd slightly forgotten they were here.

"Either way, thank you, Sadie," my dad says before heading to the bar. My brothers do the same, but their twin senses must be on alert because they both look back at the same time, smirking.

"I'm happy you had a good day," Sadie says.

Without thinking, I reach my hand forward and rest it on her knee. My thumb rubs her inner thigh as I try to think of what I'm about to say. I'm touching her as if it's something I do every day. As if touching her is the most normal thing for us.

"Enough about my day," I say. "This is your party."

"Hmm, you know what I like the most about today?" she asks.

"If you say watching me skate on the ice, I swear I'm going to—"

I close my mouth before I can finish that sentence. The things I would do to punish her would not be things my best friend approves of.

But, oh hell, these feelings aren't going away anytime soon. If ever. I should just man up and—

"You're going to what, Hudson?"

Sadie leans close, and I suck in a breath at how her presence makes me feel. Anxious and tempted all at once.

This party needs to end before I get myself into trouble.

"I can't finish that sentence,'" I tell her.

"But it's my birthday."

I chuckle. "Tell me the best part of this day."

She rolls her eyes and says, "My favorite part of this day was spending it with you."

Fuck. This woman is trying to kill me.

I'm at war with the choices I need to make, and here sits Sadie Collins, openly asking me to choose her.

"I think I'm going to take off," Brooke says rather loudly as she approaches us. Then she whispers, "Someone has to be the first to make the move."

Sadie stands to hug her goodbye, and quickly, a domino effect happens as everyone steps up to say their goodbyes for the night.

Linc and Sadie's dad are the last to leave.

"Are you sure you don't want to go home tonight?" Linc asks

her. He's talking in quiet tones, but since I've remained next to Sadie's side, I hear him loud and clear.

"Not yet."

Linc leans in to hug his sister; his gaze flickering to mine over her shoulder.

As soon as everyone is gone, I make my way to the windows to turn the blinds and start closing the place down.

"Thank you for tonight," Sadie says, following suit and speeding up the process.

"Of course."

As soon as everything is locked up, we head for the back stairs. Sadie doesn't waste time the moment we are inside my apartment with the door closed.

"Why did you do that?" she asks.

"Do what?"

"Plan a surprise party for me."

I shrug and step to move around her, but she stops me.

"Answer me."

I take a deep breath and look down into her eyes.

"I told you. I wanted a way to say thank you, and I also didn't want you to feel like you missed those years."

"Why?"

"Sadie," I warn.

"Just tell me. Tell me why you still let me live here. Tell me why you wanted me by your side when you went back to the ice rink. Tell me why you go to the store and buy food you hate just because you know I like it. And tell me why you would close your bar just to have a party for me that included maybe twenty people. Tell me, because—"

"Because I want you, Sadie," I snap. She steps back as my breathing increases. "I want you with me at all times. I want you here when I wake up, when I go to bed, when I come up for lunch to make a sandwich, when I walk to the gym, or when …

hell, Sadie, I want you every single moment of the day that I breathe. Just you. You're all I think about."

My hands are all but shaking because she's too far out of reach, and I've never once had an outburst like that. Seconds pass, and she doesn't do more than look at me.

I step toward her.

"I've never … wanted anything or *anyone* the way I want you. Not even hockey."

Her hands drop to her sides. "I think I've made it clear what I want, and you've done nothing but tell me it can't happen, so forgive me if I'm confused by your confession, Hudson."

"I know."

"So, give me the real reason you won't take what you want. Not the shitty *your brother's my best friend* excuse."

The words are on my lips, but I can't get them out.

She must feel my struggle, because Sadie moves until she's right in front of me; her left hand caresses my face.

"You can tell me."

"I'm afraid that if we start this, your memory will come back, and we'll never get to see how it ends."

She doesn't respond right away, and I can't decipher the expression in her eyes … I want to read them. I want to know her so deeply that I always know what she's thinking or feeling before she says it. I want to know her better than anyone ever before, but fuck, losing her would be my undoing.

"I think it's safe to say that my memory of who we used to be isn't coming back."

"You don't know that for sure."

She shakes her head. "No, I suppose I don't."

The room falls so eerily quiet that, even though you can hear a car idling outside or the flap of the bars sign in the wind, our breathing seems to be louder.

"Hudson."

"Yes?"

"All those things you said a moment ago, I want those, too, and I'm aware of the risk. But what if my memory doesn't come back? Then what? We wasted all this time we could have been happy together because of fear. I don't want to do that. I just want you."

I try to back away from her, but she keeps a hold of me and pulls me closer.

"Please don't," she begs. "Please."

"Sadie," I whisper as she rests her forehead on mine. "If we do this, I need you to do something for me."

"Okay," she says softly. "What is it?"

"Promise me that if your memory ever comes back, this will be the version of us you keep."

She pulls back, her hands still cupping my face. Her eyes peer into mine as if she's trying to read everything going on inside my head right now.

As if she can understand everything with one look, she kisses me softly.

"I promise."

My hands drop to grip her hips. She lets out the sexiest squeak as I jerk her closer to me.

I want her as close as she can be, and on her next breath, I crash her lips to mine.

Everything about Sadie surrounds me. Her soft skin under my fingertips, her lavender scent, the way her mouth tastes sweet like the wine she switched to downstairs, and the way her mouth feels against mine as if it was made for me.

I slip my tongue through our lips to tangle with hers, and at my touch, she throws her arms around my neck. I use this new angle to grip behind her thighs and lift her until her legs wrap around me as I walk us back to the bedroom.

Last night in the kitchen was just the beginning. This, tonight, there will be no coming back from it.

When we do this, this is it for us. I don't need to be with her to know that this woman is it for me.

I step through the doorway, her hands gripping my hair and tugging on it the way she did when my face was happily snacking between her legs. My cock grows to life, more so than when she wrapped her legs around me. She tries to pull me with her as I lay her on the bed, but I unlock her hands from around my neck, and then I step back.

She's glowing.

The smile on her face is brighter than I've ever seen, and her gaze, the way she drinks me in from head to toe, makes me jerk my belt off in one swift motion and unzip my jeans to free my erection that keeps swelling under her look.

I can't wait to make her mine.

"Take your shirt off," I tell her, reaching into my briefs and gripping myself. I pull my dick out and love how she watches the way I stroke it.

She opens her mouth to say something, but as soon as she sets her sights on the way my thumb rolls over the head, she nods and does as she's told.

"Good girl," I say as she looks at me, obediently waiting for her next order.

"Now, climb onto your knees and sit on the edge of the bed."

Again, there is no objection.

I take a step toward her, my hand continuing to move up and down my length.

"Do you want this?"

She nods.

"I need to hear you say it. Do you want this?"

"Yes."

"Where?"

A naughty gaze floats up to mine as she smirks. "In my mouth, between my legs, anywhere you want me to *take* it."

I choke on my next breath, which only causes her to grin wickedly.

"If you can talk dirty, so can I," she says.

She bites her lips, reaching for the button on her jean shorts.

"Ah, ah, I didn't say you take those off yet."

Her head falls back on a laugh, drawing my gaze to her neck.

Fuck these games right now.

I let go of myself and close the gap between me and the bed. I grab Sadie and flip her onto her back. My hand moves quickly, unzipping and pulling her clothes off her body. I grip her panties at the same time so that in one motion, she's bare to me. All that's left is her bra, which I discard just as fast.

As if we are two sex-crazed teenagers, she helps me strip from my jeans and my shirt, too. Being naked around someone for a time can be weird, but not with Sadie. I can see it with every confident movement that she feels the same. She pushes herself up and backs up to the top of the bed; I crawl over her to make sure that I'm hovering over her the entire time. Once she reaches a spot where she is most comfortable, she stops.

This time, when I kiss her, I move with patience. I kiss her as if there is nowhere in the world for me to be other than right here with her. Her mind and her body are my only focus at this moment. For tonight.

The softness of her lips and the way she circles her tongue with mine leaves me twitching to be inside her.

I nudge my legs between hers, and she opens for me, but not wide enough. I grab both of her knees, spreading her wide. I glance down to her core, and the glisten that shines back at me makes me growl.

"All this for me?" I ask.

"Keep licking your lips like that and you won't even have to touch me."

I let out a howl of a laugh and then run a finger from her calf all the way up to her thigh, following the slope that dips between her legs.

She reaches for my hand and guides me the rest of the way.

"There's no need to take your time, Hudson. You can have me again and again."

I don't reply, but I let my index finger slide inside her. She gasps, her hips rising off the bed. I adjust myself so that I can rest my other forearm on her hips to keep her in place.

Then I add a finger.

She moans.

So I add a third.

She moans louder.

"I love the noises you make," I tell her. "But I want you to sit up and watch."

"Watch? Watch what?" she asks, lifting herself to balance on her hands.

"The way you take me," I answer pulling my fingers out, sticking them in my mouth. I quickly roll a condom on and then guide my cock to her entrance. Slowly, oh so deliciously slowly, I push in.

"Fuck," I say. "You're so drenched, I thought I'd slide right in, but baby, you are tighter than I imagined."

"Oh, you feel so good."

She's closed her eyes again.

I grip just under neck and growl out, "I told you to watch."

Her eyes snap open, and she grins.

"Yes, sir."

As soon as she casts her gaze down, I push the rest of the way in. I want to stop and savor the way her pussy grips me, but I can't, I can feel her sucking me so tight that I know what she wants, what she needs. So, I pull back and slam into her. My hand is still at the base of her neck as I hammer into her.

"Yes!"

"Fuck, baby, your body loves me."

"Harder," she says, and I laugh, but do as she says.

"Oh my god, oh fuck, I'm going to …"

Her words drift off as she tries to control her breathing. Her body is clamping around me, and the pressure is like lighting a firework. My orgasm shoots down my spine and through my entire body.

I keep the pace until the feeling starts to simmer, and then I slowly pump in and out. She's humming a noise now that I swear is the only reason I'm still hard.

"Keeping making noises like that and there won't be time to rest." I capture her lips to mine.

She lets her hands go to thread them to my hair and deepen our kiss.

"What if I don't need rest?"

I kiss her once more and then pull out.

When I take in the view of her below me and the blissful smile on her face, I sure as hell hope fate won't take this away from me too.

CHAPTER TWENTY-THREE

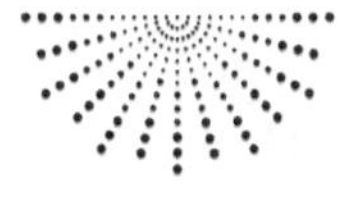

SADIE

After three weeks of living together, Hudson finally slept in his bed with me.

Sorry, couch, but it looks like you won't be seeing any more of him.

The curtains are still closed from last night, but I can see a small sliver of the morning sun trying to peek into the room.

The former baker in me—I can confidently say that now—is the first to wake up. Now, I've seen Hudson sleeping before. As the early riser, I've had moments like this before, but whereas in those moments I was tiptoeing around the apartment, trying not to wake him, and only sneaking glimpses of him, today's version of me is not hiding a single thing.

I know we fell asleep curled into each other last night, but right now, I'm on my side facing him as he faces me. Not a single body part is touching the other's.

It makes me want to laugh, because in all the books I read, the couple is always touching when they are in bed. Those novels must not have a California king bed. I'm not saying that Hudson and I didn't cuddle, but at some point, we parted ways.

But just having him be the first thing I see when I open my eyes is just as intimate.

His breaths are slow and even, and one arm is slung over his head. Look, he's sexy, but I still have this urge to reach over and tickle his armpit. What a way to wake up the day after a night filled with sex, huh?

I let out a little laugh, and even though I thought it was quiet enough, Hudson stirs.

He doesn't fully wake up, though.

I don't want to wake him either. He hasn't had the comfiness of this bed for weeks—I imagine he's going to sleep in today.

I slink out of bed, quietly change into some clothes, and then sneak down to the bakery.

I need to see what kind of documents I have in the office that can help me determine our lease so that I can get an offer for Brooke. Until this moment, I've been grateful for autopay because the bills haven't gotten behind, but if I'm going to sell this place to Brooke, I need to know more.

There's music playing when I step in through the back door. It's just after seven, so I know the shop is open and most of her products for the day are finished, minus frosting or toppings to add here and there.

I hear the chatter of voices up front, so instead of going to talk to Brooke while she's clearly busy, I step into the office and close the door slightly behind me.

There's a photo of me and my mom when I was in fifth grade on the wall above the computer, and right next to it is a photo of me and Brooke standing in front of the store. We're both smiling goofy smiles. Like most of the photos I've seen lately, I don't remember it, but it's clear I was happy.

Still, letting go of this place is what's right for me.

I wake up the computer and click around between files before I find what I'm looking for.

"What are you doing down here?" Hudson's voice startles me for the briefest moment. He's leaning in the doorway with his arms crossed. No one has ever smiled at me the way that Hudson smiles at me. My heart races.

"I should have known you were going to follow me down here."

He nods and then steps over to kiss the top of my head.

"I told you that I like to be near you, so my body knows when you leave." He grips my chin, tilts my head back, and kisses me. "So, really though, what are you doing?" he asks again.

"I was just looking at the books. Brooke has been doing so well without me."

"Does that make you sad?"

I take a breath and set the pen in my hand down.

"No. I think I'm going to see if she wants to buy this place from me."

His brow rises in shock.

It's the first time I've admitted it out loud to anyone. A part of me thinks I should be asking my father for permission, but the other part of me remembers what he said the other day: no matter what happens in my life, do everything with love. If I stayed on as the owner of the bakery, I'd be doing it out of guilt. The guilt that I gave up on my mom's dream.

But at the end of the day, it was her dream and not mine, and I'd like to think she'd approve of my choice. This bakery needs someone to run it with as much passion as she did. Brooke is that person.

"You are?"

I nod. "I don't love it the way she does. I think if I did, that passion would have come back by now."

Hudson takes a seat on the corner of the desk. He leans forward and tucks a piece of hair behind my ear.

My heart races, and I cross my legs.

So that's what that feels like.

"Is this what you want?" he asks.

"Yes."

"Then you should do it."

"What if she doesn't say yes because she's worried I'll remember one day?"

"Well, I guess we promise that you'll remember how you felt back then *and* how you feel right now."

He clears his throat and stands quickly.

He's not just talking about the bakery.

"This is Brooke we're talking about. She knows both versions of you. I think she'll love the idea."

"Really?"

"Yes, but do you know what I would love?" he asks, reaching for my hand and pulling me out of the chair. "If you'd come back to bed with me."

His nose nudges mine as I ask, "Right now?"

"Right now," he repeats.

He kisses me with so much passion that he pushes me against the desk. His hand slides to my backside and cups my butt. I feel the moment he starts to lift me, but the door swings open.

"I'm all for this, but this is a bakery. There is a legit kitchen right outside this door." Hudson pulls back, and I swear I hear a growl come from him.

"Also," Brooke goes on as she points at Hudson, "shirts are required here."

I let out a light laugh, grab his hand, and pull him to the door.

"Sorry, Boss, it won't happen again," I tease and then leave through the kitchen with Hudson right behind me.

When I look back, my best friend is grinning and shaking her head.

She waves just as we exit.

Hudson wastes no time tossing me over his shoulder.

I smack his back.

"Hey!"

"Hey, nothing," he says and opens the door to his apartment. "I said I wanted you back in my bed, and I'm making it happen."

"I can go willingly," I laugh.

"Yeah, but this way is more fun."

"It's more caveman."

He ignores my comment and sets me on my feet at the base of the stairs.

"After you," he says playfully and gestures to the stairwell.

I could stand here and just keep grinning, but when he reaches for me, I squeal and race up the steps.

His laughter is all I hear behind me.

And I love every minute of it.

———

We haven't left the apartment all day, and you will not hear me complain about it.

I think we needed this. A day for just us. To bask in what has changed between us without the pressure of the outside world.

There's no doubt my brother will have something to say, and I know that bothers Hudson.

"If you sell to Brooke, what do you think you'll do?" Hudson asks, drawing soft circles on my back. I'm just coming back down from the high of another orgasm—I've lost count of how many I've had at this point.

Still, I don't have to think over my answer.

"Is it crazy to think that even though the bar is in the spot I originally wanted Sips and Stories, I could still find another place to open it?"

"It's not crazy. I think you can."

He grins, and my heart just can't handle it. It beats faster as I lean over to kiss him.

I want all his smiles and all his kisses for as long as he'll give them to me.

He reaches up to stroke my cheek with his thumb. "What was that for?"

"For the simple fact that you listen to me, and you believe in me."

Instead of replying, he leans in to kiss me again.

"What was that for?" I ask, repeating his words.

"For reminding what it's like to be happy again."

For a moment, we just stare at each other, and then we both erupt into laughter.

"Wow, that was a sappy moment," I say.

"We seem to be having a lot of those."

I roll my eyes, push off him, and start getting dressed. We did pause to eat breakfast, but we skipped lunch, and I'm ravenous.

"But seriously, do you think I can do it? Sell the bakery and open my own place?"

"I do," he says and steps into his briefs. "Tell me what you think it would look like."

"Well, I still like the idea of mostly windows for the walls."

He pulls on a shirt and then tosses me one of his to wear over my leggings. It swallows me, but I love it.

He heads for the door of the room, stopping only to gently press his lips to mine.

"I like the idea of windows too."

"It's not too lame to want it to look like the bar's space? I just kept dreaming of that, and it's hard to ignore it."

"It's not weird. If there were another option for the bar, I'd trade you."

"Really?" I take a seat at the small kitchen island in his kitchen.

"Of course."

"Hmm, this all feels too good to be true." I tap my chin as he turns to face me.

"What does?"

"You."

He chuckles. "Well, believe it, Sadie Baby, because you chose me."

He places a hand on either side of me and traps me between his arms as he leans down for another kiss. It lingers, and he moves to step between my legs. It takes all I have to push him back.

"I need food," I tell him. "But also, I like Sadie Baby a lot better than the last nickname you gave me."

"I've never given you a nickname."

"Yes, you have."

"What nickname was that?" he asks and goes back to pulling out the ingredients for sandwiches.

"Sadie Snots."

His head jerks to look at me. "I never called you that."

"You, mister, started the rumor for it back in high school."

He shakes his head. "Nope. That wasn't me. The first person I heard call you that was Amber."

"Amber?" My ex-best friend whom Hudson dated his senior year? We remained friends until we graduated a couple of years later, but she kept sleeping with my boyfriends.

"Yeah. She was mad that Parker Basin was taking you to prom. She thought she was the only sophomore invited by a senior."

I narrow my gaze at him.

"She told me you started it."

He spreads the mayo on the bread but pauses. "I think we all learned she wasn't very trustworthy."

I nod. "Huh. I've held a grudge against you for that one for a while. Parker wouldn't even kiss me that night. I had to wait an entire year until I got my first one. With tongue, anyway."

"Who was it?" Hudson snaps, staring at me intently. "Was it that soccer loser, Buddy?"

I laugh and shake my head. "I'm not going to tell you."

"Tell me," he demands, abandoning the food and marching over to me. He spins me in my chair and cages me again.

"Nope."

"Sadie," he says.

I press a hand to his lips. "I think you mean Sadie *Baby*."

Now it's his gaze that narrows on me. He clears his throat.

"Sadie Baby, tell me who your first kiss was, now."

"Or what?"

In one swift motion, he grabs my left thigh, pulls it up to his hip, and brushes himself against me. His erection hits me right at my core, and I groan.

"I can hold out," he teases.

I reach a hand between us and cup him.

"Can you?"

He answers with a hard kiss, and then, as if it's just a typical Sunday, the two of us are stripped naked in a matter of minutes.

Without taking his lips from mine, he moves us to the couch, where he sits down, pulling me to sit on his lap. I rest a leg on each side of him and reach to place him at my entrance.

He stops my hand.

"I need to get a condom."

"I'm ... okay without one if you are. I'm clean."

"I am too."

His blue eyes settle on mine, and today they seem lighter. Calmer. And it makes me fall for him even more knowing that I make him feel the way he makes me feel.

I lower slightly, letting my body adjust to his size before I slide down fully.

He bites my shoulder when I'm all the way seated.

"Fuck, you feel so good."

I turn his face to me so that I can kiss him.

He deepens it with his tongue and then grips my hips and starts to move me back and forth; I know I won't last long.

And I don't.

I'm shattering in his arms within minutes, and he's right behind me.

But that's okay, because there will be many more nights for this.

For us.

This right here, this bond Hudson and I have—nothing can take it away from us.

CHAPTER TWENTY-FOUR

HUDSON

The last week has been a blur. If I haven't been working at the bar and Sadie hasn't been working on her ideas for Sips and Stories, we've been holed up in my apartment.

Mostly naked, a little tired, but definitely happier than I've been in years.

Which is how I ended up where I am now.

Sunday morning breakfast used to be a thing back when I was a kid. My mom would make a huge spread of dishes. She'd have bacon, sausage, eggs both cheesy scrambled and over easy, toast, pancakes, and fruit. She'd wake up before everyone else and make sure the table was set before we all woke up. It never occurred to me at the time, but now that I'm older, I've realized that it sure as hell could not have been easy, let alone cheap, to raise three boys.

I put my truck in park outside of my dad's house and take notice that both Miles's and Luca's vehicles are already here.

It doesn't take a rocket scientist to notice that even though I left and changed over the years, and even though our mom is no longer with us, the tradition is still alive and well with my family.

Honestly, I was hoping this is what I'd show up to.

After I first moved back home, Luca sent a text to me every Saturday night to remind me of this. That went on for about three months before the messages stopped.

Hell, I've been a shitty brother and son for the last three years. If Sadie has taught me anything in the last month, it's that it's never too late to make amends.

I grab the bag of donuts and the dish of spinach and egg quiche Sadie whipped up this morning that I brought with me.

When I told her the story of Sunday breakfast, I didn't think she would read so much into it, but as it's been extremely clear, she simply just keeps surprising me.

I don't knock on the front door. Instead, I walk in only to freeze. Luca, Miles, and my father are all sitting at the table. Their gazes quickly shift to me.

I brace myself for some smart-ass comments or "it's about damn time" teasing, but my dad just smiles as Luca says, "That better be Sadie's cooking and not yours."

It's a tease, but not the one I was expecting.

I hold up the bag. "And Brooke's donuts, fresh from this morning."

Miles jumps up and yanks the bag out of my hand as I set the quiche on the table to go with their bacon and eggs.

"Chocolate glazed, hell yes."

Then, as if my being here isn't something out of the ordinary, they continue their conversation. I take my seat, and Dad hands me a plate and fork without a word.

"So, if she isn't going to hire you to do the rebuild for them, who is she going to hire?" Miles directs his question at Luca.

"Fuck if I know. I told her it would be twice as expensive if she hired someone who wasn't local, but she said, and I quote,

I'd pay any amount of money if the result is that I don't have to see your arrogant face every single day."

Miles bursts into deep laughter while my dad shakes his head.

"Who are we talking about?" I ask, plating up some quiche and passing the dish to Luca.

"Shay Parker."

"Shay Parker, as in Leo Parker's little sister, Shay?"

"That's the one." Luca blows out a breath.

Leo Parker has been a sore subject for Luca since his sophomore year of high school. From first grade, it was Leo and Luca, troublemakers and best friends till the end. Until they weren't. Leo was the one friend Luca and Miles didn't fight over. It was like everyone knew Leo and Luca were a one-of-a-kind duo.

I tried to coax him to tell me why they aren't friends anymore, but Luca went with the standard "we just grew apart" answer.

Which is a load of shit if you ask me, considering they have both gone on to thrive in their careers and are both well-known and cared for by the people here in Lovers. Luca runs the construction company that does all the work in Lovers, and Leo is one of two Parker kids who have taken over running the marina by the lake.

That said, Luca's company has done all the remodels around town for almost all the businesses here, so why is this one different?

"She never objected to using your company before," I say, and all of them turn to me.

"We need to catch you up," Miles shakes his head. "The last remodel was four years ago while Mr. Parker still owned the place."

"O-kay."

I sense there's more.

"Shay moved back about a year before you did once she graduated with her business degree. After Shay took over, the building hasn't needed much, give or take a few repairs here and there. Those are single day jobs Shay can easily avoid Luca with."

I nod. I'm aware that each Parker kid was required to attend school and get a degree in the field they wanted to manage when it came to the marina. Their father was very clear that he would sell or hire others who were more capable. If his kids wanted to continue the family business, they had to earn it.

So, it seems Shay did her part and is now back and making the rules.

"And she won't hire you because …"

"Fuck if I know," Luca spits. "Because her brother hates me, so she does by association."

"Really, I would think that since you and her—"

"You know what, let's talk about something happy, yeah? So, you and Sadie are getting close?" Luca cuts me off, and I can't help but laugh.

That is, to his point, a much happier topic. Yet it's still one I'm not sure how to answer outside of the standard *yes*. I guess all I can hope for is that they don't ask any follow-up questions.

But even I know that the chances of that are low.

"Well, we definitely aren't fighting like we used to."

"I can't believe she got you to go back to the rink," Miles says.

I nod.

"Onto the actual ice," Dad adds. It's a statement not a question, but still, I keep nodding.

"How was it different for her compared to us trying to help you?" Luca asks. The softness in his voice tells me he genuinely wants to know and that he isn't mad. He tried harder than anyone else. The difference is simple: He's not Sadie.

"We drove by the rink when we went to go get the new couch in Wind Valley a couple of weeks ago. She was out of the truck and basically running to the door before I caught her. I wasn't about to let her go skating with a head injury like hers. By the time we got to the doors, I confessed I hadn't been in a rink since the accident, and she just stood there with me until I made a choice."

None of them speak, but their eager eyes tell me they want me to go on.

"I guess I just thought that here I was choosing to pretend my past didn't exist, and all the while I was standing next to a woman who would give anything to remember hers."

Luca nods. "So, you went in."

"Yes. The high school team was just exiting the locker room, and suddenly not only had I stepped foot into the rink, but I had kids wanting to talk hockey and asking for tips. It was surreal. It was nothing like I expected."

"I'm glad Sadie was there. She's been good for you," Dad says quickly. He clears his throat—it's his tell-tale sign that he's getting emotional. Talk fast and clear his throat after.

"I think she might be a little too good for me," I admit.

Miles starts to chuckle. "Good. It's about time you figure it out."

"Why don't you look happy about it?" Luca asks.

I let out a breath. God, I'm getting sentimental, but these are my people. No matter how much I pushed them away, they have always been here, and they will always be here. So, it only seems fitting that I tell them exactly how I feel so that I won't be alone in this again.

"Because … I was in love with hockey, and it was taken from me in seconds. I'm afraid that if I let myself feel too much for Sadie, and her memory comes back, it'll be the same."

I'll lose the one thing that I care most about in this world.

Of course, I don't tell them that part.

They can put it together.

Miles lets out a puff of air. "That's the most you've said to us about your life since you got back."

"So, are you saying that you're in love with Sadie?" Dad asks.

My gaze flashes to him, and then Luca chuckles.

"Shit, she's only been living with you for a few weeks. That was fast."

I shake my head and run a hand down the front of my face.

"It's something," I say and then refuse to fight the grin.

"What does Linc think?" Miles asks.

My smile slips.

"He doesn't know."

"He doesn't know that you like his sister?"

"He doesn't know a lot," I reply.

Dad chuckles and gets up. "You'd better tell him. He's your best friend."

"I know. It just … he asked me to help her, and now we're … I don't even know what we are."

"Are you planning on having a fling with her?" Luca asks.

"What? No. Why would you ask that?"

"Because if you're not, then you need to tell him, and you need to tell him before he finds out from someone else. He won't like that you're hiding this from him."

"I'm not hiding this. I'll tell him. I just want to make sure the timing is right."

"Anytime is the right time," Dad says from the kitchen.

I know he's right.

I nod, and the conversation switches to more work talk between Luca's company and the garage Miles owns. Last summer, he built a house behind it on some property that he bought, and they just finished the apartment that's attached to the side of the garage. The plan is that someday Dad will move into it, but until then, Miles is considering renting it out.

The rest of breakfast is uneventful, but one thing is for sure by the time I'm backing out of the driveway and heading home.

I'll be back next week and many more after that.

I pull into my parking spot behind the bar, pop inside to check on the staff, and then head upstairs.

I can smell my apartment before I open the door. The lemon scent that fills the stairwell makes my stomach growl, which is saying something, because I just ate my weight in food at my dad's.

Sadie doesn't hear me when I open the door. She's in the kitchen, the counters are a mess, and she's swaying side to side as Laney Wilson plays through my little Bluetooth speaker.

I take this moment to watch her.

The way she moves around this place as if she owns it, the way her things are scattered around as if this has always been her home, the way my heart swells as I think about how I never want to come home and not find her here.

She spins, and as soon as she sees me, a smile breaks out on her lips.

"You're home. How did it go?"

"Good," I say and wrap my hands around her hips, then lean against the counter as I pull her to me.

She grins, setting down the spatula that was in her hand and wrapping her arms around my neck.

"I'm happy to hear that." She presses a light kiss to my lips. "Was it my quiche?"

I nod. "Definitely."

"I thought so."

She nods again firmly, as if she knew it would be her cooking, and then backs up.

"I made you lemon bars."

"I can see that. I thought you didn't like baking."

"I like baking. I just don't want to do it for a living."

"Ah."

I glance around the small kitchen, a lump forming in my throat.

She made me lemon bars.

"I wasn't sure how it was going to go today, so I wanted you to have something special when you got back just in case, and you told me a while back that these are your favorite, so"—she tosses her hands up—"I just made them."

My favorite.

Fuck.

I need to tell her that she was making these the night she fell. Am I the reason she was there? I'll never know, but I need to tell her.

"I have something to tell you," I say and then rub the back of my neck.

Her gaze snaps to mine, and she stands a little taller.

"Okay. You look tense. Am I not going to like this?"

"I ... I don't know."

"Does it have anything to do with us?"

I nod.

"The us before or after I hit my head?"

Dread sprints through my entire body.

What if I tell her about this and it sparks her memory? All of it. Then, suddenly, we'll be back to where we started.

Shit.

Shit.

"Well?" she prompts me.

I have to tell her. I have to.

"The night you hit your head, you were making lemon bars."

She studies me for a moment.

"Okay."

"And … the day before that, I told you that your lemon bars were subpar and that I had to wash them down with beer, or some version of that."

I swear my entire body is pulsing with each beat of my heart as I wait for her to reply.

She crosses her arms but doesn't say anything.

"And so, you think that I was there that night because of you?"

I give one single nod and wait.

Instantly, her expression softens, and she steps toward me, reaches up to run her fingers through my hair, and kisses me.

"I have no doubt that I was there trying to perfect something someone told me wasn't my best, but you didn't push me down, Hudson. What happened wasn't your fault."

"You were there because of me. I'm sure of it."

"We don't know that. Either way, you are not the reason I hit my head. Listen," she says and turns my face to look at her, "you are not responsible for what happened to me. All right?"

How can she be so accepting of everything right now?

"All right?" she repeats. "Tell me you hear me."

"I hear you."

"Good."

She presses to her toes and kisses me.

"Now let's eat these yummy bars, get naked, and then possibly start brainstorming ideas for locations for Sips and Stories."

She retreats to the kitchen quickly, and the guilt that vanished right away when she told me the accident wasn't my fault is back. I should tell her that she wants Mrs. Whittaker's space. I should tell her about the deal we made to decide who gets it, but what if I tell her, she remembers, and then boom, she pushes her dream of Sips and Stories to the back of her mind all over again to pursue what she thought she wanted before she hit her head?

Fuck.

My mind races with what choice I should make, but then she smiles at me and tells me she thinks her bookstore should be focused on romance books and starts to tell me more about the decor she wants.

I don't want her to pass up her dream again.

But that only eases my choice not to tell her about the space a little bit.

I know I'll have to tell her, just not yet.

CHAPTER TWENTY-FIVE

SADIE

"I love the view you have out here," I say as soon as I pour myself a cup of coffee and meet Hudson outside on the patio off the kitchen.

I haven't seen him sit out here very often, so when I saw him this morning, I wanted to jump at the idea of joining him—even if all I'm wearing is his T-shirt from last night.

Just the two of us, up early and enjoying our morning coffee while the town wakes up below us. The remnants of the local Fourth of July festival still line the streets from last night. The actual holiday festival for tourists happened last week over the real holiday, but our town loves to put one together for the locals. Any excuse, really.

Hudson has a booth for the bar at every festival, but from what I've seen the last few weeks, he lets his employees do all the face-to-face work.

"Yeah, I should come out here more. But I usually work so late that I miss the sunrise or the sunset. Sitting out here in the dead heat of the middle of the day just doesn't give me the same vibes."

"I don't imagine it does."

I sip my coffee and watch him.

His gaze drifts to where Bartley, Marty, and Phil are walking down the street toward us, most likely headed for the bakery. Brooke told me that each time they show up, they ask for me.

I'm ready to move on, but whenever someone tells me something like that, it makes me think I'm acting too quickly. I mean, I gave myself a month to remember and I still haven't; now I just want to continue moving on. But what if I move on too fast and miss something? How do I know when the time is right?

"How did you know you wanted to open the bar?" I ask.

Hudson looks at me slowly, a lazy smile touching his lips. My question probably seems out of the blue to him.

He reaches down, grabs my chair leg, and pulls me until we are side by side.

"Your mind is hard at work already, huh?"

I nod.

"I just want to make sure I'm making the right choice and not rushing anything."

"You think selling the bakery is rushing?"

I shrug. "Maybe. I know what I want to do, but what if I'm missing something on why I took over?"

He nods slowly. "I opened the bar because I needed a distraction."

"Oh."

"That's not the glamorous answer you were looking for, but I knew if I was moving back home, I would need to stay busy. When I was looking for a place to live, the bar popped up, and it was pretty much a two-for-one for me. I could stay busy and not live with my dad again."

"Is that what you think of it now?"

"Oh no, not even close. I like what I do. I like giving the locals and tourists a laid-back space to be in. I even like the things you've done to the place. It makes me think I need to remodel a little."

"Really?"

He nods. "People like the seating area you made. I need more of them."

"Oh, you could buy that space from Mrs. Whittaker and expand it. Make that entire side comfortable seating. Oh, and add bookshelves! It would be fun. You could have sections based on drink names. Like, the spicy section could be tequila something, and the … why are you looking at me like that?"

"Because that right there is why I don't think you're rushing the sale of the bakery. You don't talk about it the way you talk about your Sips and Stories idea."

"I wasn't talking about Sips and Stories. I was talking about your bar. Although, it would be a cute idea to combine the bar and my idea. It would mean I still get my dream and so do you."

Like before, he just stares at me with a dazed look in his eyes.

I'm boring him and totally steamrolling his bar plans and just assuming I'll be in his future. I'm probably overwhelming him.

"I know. I'm sorry."

"What?" he asks as I turn away.

"I was getting carried away and overstepped on your plans for the bar."

He sets his mug down and then slinks out of his chair down to his knees. He kneels in front of me, wrapping his arms around my waist as he looks up at me.

"People can see up here," I whisper as if they can hear us too.

"Who? The Three's Company regulars who are probably sitting on the bench outside the bakery and can't see us?"

I let out a laugh that makes him smile even more.

"I wasn't thinking that you overstepped," he goes on. "I was thinking about how much I love having you here."

"Oh."

"And I think you should move in with me."

I kiss his forehead and then laugh.

"Um, what do you call the last month?"

"I mean permanently."

I study him for a moment, his lazy smile, the way his bedhead is combed over from my hands running through it.

"You really want that?"

"I do."

I don't even take a moment to think it over. "Okay. yes."

He pushes up and kisses me.

"I guess this means we finally need to tell your brother."

My face scrunches up.

"I know."

"He's not going to be happy with me."

"No, but he should be happy *for* you."

He nods, but I see the doubt in his eyes.

I reach down and cup the side of his face.

"It's going to be okay. We've got this."

I press my lips to his softly. They brush against his once, twice, and then he rises to his feet, pulling me up with him. His hands come to my neck as he backs us up to the door, never letting our lips lose their connection. Once we're back inside, he closes the door and the curtains.

"We don't have time for this," I remind him. "You'll need to get to the bar soon."

"I have hours, and there is *always* time for this."

And then he spins me quickly and bends me over the arm of the couch.

"Looks like you picked a couch with the perfect height."

I smile, looking back at him over my shoulder.

He smirks as I bite my lip.

"Sadie, baby, you know how it makes me feel when you bite that lip."

I push back so that my ass grinds on his hard-on.

"Jealous?"

He growls, rears his hand back, and then spanks me.

My eyes widen with shock.

Jesus.

I was not expecting that.

My reaction causes him to smirk.

Instead of taking the time to shed our clothes, he drops his shorts to his feet and reaches between my legs to move my panties to the side.

I moan the moment he rubs his thumb over me, my wetness coating his fingers when they dip inside of me.

"Stop teasing me, Hudson. I want you inside me."

"A needy Sadie might be my new favorite." He leans forward so that his chest rests against my back. "Lucky for you, I'm a fan of giving you what you want."

He positions himself just right and slams into me.

"Oh god," I cry out. "Yes."

He pulls back and repeats the motion. Over and over again he pounds into me from behind. My hips hit the couch, but luckily, it's soft.

Outside of our breathing, my cries of pure bliss are the only sounds in the apartment.

"I'll never get enough of this with you," he says, slowing his movement. I peek over my shoulder to see why, only to find him watching himself.

The way he slides in and out, there is no doubt his cock is glistening with the evidence of how we make each other feel.

"What do you like best?" I ask, and his gaze snaps up to me.

His sapphire eyes turn dark as he grins.

"This part."

He pushes in to the hilt and then steadily fucks me as one hand moves around to my front and presses to my clit.

I combust on cue and scream his name.

"The way you crumble under my touch and call out my name. It's like a drug to me."

He continues to pump inside me even after my orgasm is over.

"I'm so close, baby, don't move," he says, but I don't listen. Instead, I back up, pushing him with me, and then I spin to face him, dropping to my knees.

"Holy shit," he breathes as I wrap a hand around his large erection and guide him into my mouth.

I suck hard and pulse my hand fast over him.

"Shit. Shit, I'm about to come," he says and pulls back.

I watch as he finishes himself off in his hand, his eyes still on mine as I sit on my knees.

This isn't the moment for life-changing epiphanies, but I'll be damned if watching him fall apart under my control doesn't spark something inside me.

I have the power to make my life the way I want despite what I can't remember.

Looks like I'm getting everything I wanted after all, and it starts with moving in with Hudson.

CHAPTER TWENTY-SIX

HUDSON

"You know, I think we should talk to your dad and brother before you start packing any more of your things to bring to our place."

She grins. "I like it when you call it our place."

Sadie goes back to pulling more clothes from her closet. We're going on a hike today, but first we decided to stop and get more of her things from her dad's house. Stopping before meant no one would be here, and Sadie liked that idea best. It meant fewer questions.

We haven't exactly figured out how to tell Linc about us. Her father, sure, he'll be fine, but Linc is … more sensitive.

I'm pretty sure he's going to slam his fist into my face, and Sadie is convinced he's going to go on and on about how she shouldn't be making these choices right now.

As adults, we both agreed that we should just get over it and tell him right away. As his sister and best friend, we want to wait and choose the right time.

We have dinner here tonight, so as of this moment, that's the plan.

"What do you think of this dress?" she asks and holds it up to her body.

It's a little black dress she wore last summer to one of the festival nights. It hits her about midthigh, and the fabric from just below her butt to her thighs is nothing but lace.

I noticed it on her last year and didn't say a word. I just suffered in silence.

I grin. "The last time I saw you wear that, I wished that we were more than just enemies," I admit.

She laughs. "Really? And you didn't say anything?"

"No. You spoke first and told me that I was serving stale beer, so naturally, I wasn't about to compliment how stunning you looked."

"There you go again, showing me that you've been secretly pining over me for years."

She walks to the suitcase laying open next to me on her bed, folds the dress, and sets it inside.

Before she can move back to the closet, I grab her hand and pull her back. She lands on me, so I roll us until she's on her back. Then I kiss her.

Her hands wrap around my waist, sliding to my rear. She places one leg on each side of my hips and pushes her hands into my butt as I settle on top of her.

I'd only meant to kiss her, but the sparkle in her eyes tells me she has other plans.

And even though my mind is still blown from when she hit her knees this morning, and I will happily let her do anything to me she wants, we should stop.

"Sadie, baby, I cannot do this at your dad's house."

She pulls me back down and kisses me again.

"Yes, you can."

"It's wrong. This is his home."

"It was mine once, too, and I've never had a boy in here before. It would be a first for me."

"Really?" This woman is too good for me. "You didn't bring one boyfriend into this room until me?"

A sly grin touches her lips.

"Are you calling yourself my boyfriend?"

I don't even hesitate. I will leave no question. We are exclusive.

"Yes."

"Good," she says and kisses me again.

As soon as she slips her tongue into my mouth and moans, my cock stirs to life between us. I grind into her to let her know exactly what she does to me. Not that it's a surprise at this point. These past couple of weeks since we started this new side of us, anytime she's around me, I'm ready. I can't get enough of her.

I smooth my hand up her thigh, hooking her leg to my hip, and then slide my hand to the inside of her leg. I slip it inside the bottom of her shorts and find her soaking when I reach her panties.

"I love that you are just as ready for me as I am for you."

She sits up a little and unbuttons my jeans.

"I wouldn't want you any other way."

Her hand dips into my boxers, and as soon as she grips me, I glide two fingers inside her.

She moans. "Take my shorts off."

I do as I'm told, yanking her panties off with them. She's wearing one of my shirts again, so when I flip us over to put her on top, her entire body is covered. I grab the bottom to peel off her shirt, but she pulls me out and places me at her entrance a lot faster.

"I don't have a condom with me," I tell her. We've been pretty reckless lately, and as much as I love her bare, we need to be more careful.

"It's fine. I'll hop off and finish you with my hand or my mouth," she says. "I know how you like that."

I don't have time to reply with a *fuck yes* before she's sinking onto me.

"Fuck, baby," I groan and grip her hips.

"God, I love this feeling," she says and drops her head back as she rides me. "Hudson, you are—"

"What the fuck is going on!"

Sadie and I both freeze, snapping our attention to her doorway, which is now filled with her brother's red face and clenched fists.

"Linc!" Sadie shrieks and collapses against me. I'm still inside her when she says, "Get out of my room!"

"This is fucked up!" he snaps back and slams the door. "Get out here. Right now! My eyes—fuck, I think I'm blind!"

"Shit," she whispers, her forehead still resting against my chest. "How mad do you think he is?"

"Right fucking now!" Linc yells again.

"Pretty mad," I reply.

"Yeah."

"Babe?"

"Yes?"

"As much as I love being inside you, I'm going to need you to get off me while we go talk to your brother."

She starts to laugh but gets up and finds her shorts.

"This isn't funny," I tell her.

"It's a little funny. I mean, what are the odds?"

I can't help but warm at the carefree look on her face.

I laugh too.

"You two better not be fucking laughing!" Linc yells through the door.

I roll my eyes, then zip my pants, leaving her to put herself together.

I open the door.

Linc's face is even more red as he glares at me.

"Hey, man." I lean against the closed door.

"Fuck. You—" he says and walks off down the hall. I'm hot on his heels as he steps out the front door.

"Linc, stop. Let's talk about this."

"My sister!" he yells.

"I know."

"My sister!"

"Yes."

Then he pauses, and I almost run into him.

"That's my sister!"

Oh hell, we've broken him.

"I know she is, Linc, but she's so much more than that to me."

He continues to shake his head at me.

"I asked you to help her, Hudson. Keep her stress-free. Not … not …" His hand flies up to gesture at the house. "Not whatever the hell that was. Fuck!"

"I did help her, Linc. I helped her the best that I could, but you know what else happened? She helped me. She made me a better man in just weeks, Linc. How could I not fall for her?"

"You've known her for years, and now, *now* you two decide that you should be more. Five weeks ago, you two couldn't even be in the same room. Hell, no one could be in the same room as you two, and now you're … fuck."

"You need to calm down," I say in a calmer tone.

I want to yell back, but I'm not.

"Don't fucking tell me to calm down, Hudson. This is not okay. She doesn't remember your past! Not all of it. It's not fair to her that you're tri—"

"If the remainder of that sentence is you accusing me of tricking your sister, I will not feel even an ounce of guilt for punching you right now. I did not trick her. I tried to avoid this. I tried harder than you think, but she changed me. She fixed me. She fucking brought me back to life, Linc. How the hell was I not going to fall in love with someone who would do that for me?"

His head jerks back as if I did, in fact, punch him in the face.

"You love her?"

I don't hesitate.

"Yes."

"Like *love,* love her? Love her enough to spend the rest of your life with her, love?"

I nod and then I smile.

"If she lets me."

He scowls at me for another couple of seconds, then his hands hit his hips, and he drops his chin to his chest.

"This is not how I expected my day to go."

"Day?" I question with a laugh. "Try summer. If you would have asked me if I saw myself living to make that woman smile" —I point at his dad's house—"I'd have laughed in your face."

Finally, Linc chuckles. "It's weird, but I should have seen it coming. I knew something was up at my dad's that one day, but I trusted you two."

"To be fair, nothing had happened at that point. Nothing happened until the day that—"

"The fewer details, the better, man."

"Noted."

The door swings open, and Sadie comes running out.

"Linc, you better not be ... you're not fighting?"

She looks back and forth between us as if she's unsure what to do next.

"No, we aren't fighting." I grab her hand.

Linc groans. "I might not want to kick you in the junk anymore, but that doesn't mean I'm ready for all this."

His hand waves us up and down, and then he spins. "I need to get back to work."

"Wait," Sadie calls out. "Why are you here?"

"Shit. I came to get Dad's portfolio. He forgot it."

Linc turns back for the house as I pull Sadie into my arms.

"I can't believe that just happened. How did you calm him down so fast?"

"I just told him the truth."

"And that is?"

"That I've never been happier in my entire life than when I'm with you."

Sadie pushes to her toes and presses a kiss to my mouth. I slide my tongue past her lips, igniting the passion we'd had moments ago before we were interrupted.

"I said wait till I'm gone!" Linc yells as he walks past us with their father's bag in his hand. "And you two are telling Dad tonight at dinner. Be here at six."

"You got it," I say and then kiss Sadie's forehead.

"And Sadie"—he stops to look at his sister—"by no means does this mean I'll stop worrying about you."

She rolls her eyes.

"I know."

And then her brother is gone, and it's just the two of us again.

She laughs. "Well, now that's over, it looks like things are smooth sailing from here for us."

She beams and then turns back to the house.

Yeah.

Smooth sailing.

CHAPTER TWENTY-SEVEN

SADIE

Today is a big day for me.

I've put together the proposal for Brooke, and I'm headed to the bakery to pitch her the idea after it closes in about twenty minutes.

My heart is hammering in my chest as I descend the stairs.

Selling the bakery is the first step to making Sips and Stories a reality. Turns out, I need the money from the sale to buy a place. I have a good chunk in savings, thanks to living with my dad, but not enough.

I'm pretty convinced that I couldn't afford the space where the bar is, but I also wasn't prepared to sell the bakery at that time, so I moved in with my dad to take care of him and save money while putting my dreams on the back burner.

It's the only logical sequence.

But now, things have changed, and in a twisted way, hitting my head and forgetting the last three years might be the best thing that ever happened to me.

I make my way through the bakery's kitchen and into the

seating area quickly, finding Brooke laughing with a table of tourists.

She spots me right away and waves.

The women she'd been chatting with leave shortly after, and Brooke joins me at another table.

"It's been so busy in here lately. I love it," she beams. "How are you?"

"I'm great."

"Oh no, you have a look. What's wrong?"

"Nothing." I give her my best smile. "I have something I want to talk to you about."

"Okay," she says slowly.

There isn't really an easy way to say this, so I just blurt it out.

"I want you to buy the bakery from me."

"What?" Her brows nearly hit her hairline. "No. This was your mom's place, and she loved it. I'm not family. I would be—"

"The person I know she would pick to take over."

Brooke's bottom lip wobbles as she studies me.

"But what about you? What will you do?"

I grin even bigger. She isn't arguing to say no again.

"I'm going to open Sips and Stories."

"Seriously! Finally." She claps. "You've been talking about it for years, but I wasn't sure how dedicated you were to the idea. You said it was a blip of an idea before your mom passed."

"Well, it's happening now. As soon as I sell you this place."

She tries to hold back her smile.

"You really want me to buy it?"

"Do you want to buy it?"

She glances around slowly and then nods quickly. "I love it here."

"Perfect. I have an offer here, but remember, this part is business, so if you don't like it, you need to make me a counteroffer."

"Oh, look at the little Realtor blood in you shining bright."

She takes the folder from me and then gets up to lock the register.

"I already closed up the back, so you want to walk out with me?"

"I would love to."

My voice is extra cheery, but how can it not be? Step one is complete. I can't wait to tell Hudson. Brooke is locking the door just as Mrs. Whittaker appears.

"Hi, Mrs. Whittaker." I wave as she steps out of the space she's been trying to sell. After all these years of her saying she wouldn't sell it, I would have assumed that someone would be eager to buy the space.

Perhaps everything has been happening for a reason. Maybe this new direction in life has brought me to this moment. It might not be the original space I planned for Sips and Stories, but I have this giddy feeling that it's going to be better.

I should buy this space.

"Hi, Sadie, how are you doing today?"

"I'm well, thank you."

I glance into the window and notice the for sale sign is down. Oh no.

"Did someone buy this place?" I ask. I do my best to hide the disappointment in my tone. She wasn't aware I wanted it. No one was since the thought just came to my mind. I can't fault her for anything.

She eyes me as if she's thinking over her next words carefully.

"Yes. I sold the spot," Mrs. Whittaker says. Her gaze shifts to Brooke and then back to me. "I thought you knew that."

"How would I know that?" I ask.

"Because you and Hudson both came to me a little over a month ago to buy it. I told you two to become friends and pick which one of you gets it. He signed the paper this morning, and I'll admit, I was shocked when he put—"

"Hudson knew I wanted this place?" I interrupt her.

She nods. "Yes, but he also—"

"He also—" I repeat, but out of nowhere, I feel like I've been hit in the gut.

I suck in a breath. I can see the two of us, me and Hudson, standing in the space fighting, of Mrs. Whittaker telling us her rules, of him telling me he hates my mom's lemon bars. Me at the funeral. Me finding out he bought the bar and that he moved into the apartment above it. The way he'd look at me like it disgusted him to even be near me. Like he could never see me as anything other than the enemy. Like I was someone who did nothing but stand in the way of him getting what he wants.

I remember everything.

CHAPTER TWENTY-EIGHT

HUDSON

I leave the bank with a grin on my face and hop into my truck to head to my brother's place. He isn't at his office today, but he still has what I need.

I'd planned to make a whole spectacle of telling Sadie about this, but in the end, just having a moment for the two of us is what she'd love the most.

Luca is grabbing something from his truck when I pull up.

"I can't believe you bought the space and put her name as co-owner," Luca says. "Can you even do that?"

I'm not even surprised by that greeting.

"She still needs to sign the paperwork, but yeah. It's done. Mrs. Whittaker said she'd take down the sign today."

"Fuck, I can't believe this. This summer has been wild to watch."

I head for his front door. I can't wait to tell Sadie. She's going to be so excited. As soon as she mentioned adding a book-store to the bar the other morning, my decision was a no-brainer. I'll get the space from Mrs. Whittaker, and we can remodel both spaces to make both of our dreams work. I just wanted to get the paperwork in line before I told Sadie in case it didn't work out the way I wanted.

But now, all is good.

I'm not sure how much she'll like the idea of breaking down the walls to make one big space, but if she wants Sips and Stories by the big windows, we will need to move all the tables and the section of the bar on that side to the space I just bought. If she wants it, I'll add her name to the bar's legal paperwork, too.

"Do you think she's going to freak out?" Luca asks as he shows me a couple of mock-up designs.

Since Luca does the majority of the construction in our town, of course I hired him to draft me a plan for how we could make this work. I'd called him that same day to get a couple of blueprints going.

"No," I answer with complete confidence.

"You're that sure about her?"

"Yes."

He chuckles. "A month ago, I would not have believed this. It's just mind-blowing."

"You've told me this before. Can I take these?" I point at his blueprints. "I want to show them to Sadie when I tell her today."

"You're going now?" His eyes look like they are about to pop out of their sockets.

"Yeah."

I've waited long enough.

"Jesus, Hud. One day you were avoiding all things that involve other people, and now—"

"And now I'm done letting life pass me by."

My brother claps his hands like a kid on Christmas morning and follows me to the door. "I'm coming with you."

I roll my eyes, but I don't tell him no.

Turns out, I've missed the way my brothers and I used to be connected at the hip.

We get in my truck and drive into town. I park in front of the bar, my gaze instantly finding Sadie outside the bakery.

Just seeing her is like a dose of serotonin.

I jump out of the truck, the thrill of telling her that I have plans for my life again racing through my veins.

I haven't been this excited about something since hockey, and I know it's all thanks to her.

"Ladies," I say, greeting Mrs. Whittaker, Brooke, and Sadie. Sadie has her back to me, so I walk up ready to scoop her into my arms and share my good news, but Brooke's gaze catches mine. I slow my steps just as Sadie turns around.

Her eyes are red, and her cheeks are wet from tears.

The caramel eyes I've grown to love and wake up to look back at me with an emotion I can't place.

But her gaze is detached.

My heart drops and my stomach turns as we stare at each other.

She doesn't need to say the words. I know she remembers it all.

"I'm sorry, Hudson," Mrs. Whittaker says quietly. She squeezes my arms. "I thought she knew." Then, she quietly walks away and gets in her car.

I heard her, and I can hear my brother mumbling behind me, but I ignore them all, never letting my gaze leave Sadie's.

I swallow, licking my lips and glancing at the building for a split second before returning to her.

I'm not sure where to start, so I wait for her to speak first.

But it seems she has the same idea, because after another minute of silence passes, she turns with a huff.

"Sadie, wait," I call out and reach for her.

"For what, Hudson? So you can trick me into getting what you want again?"

"What?" I ask, my head rearing back like she slapped me. "Trick you? I didn't trick you."

"Oh, yeah, so you just conveniently forgot that Mrs. Whittaker told us we had to become friends and choose who gets to buy this space. Or did you forget to tell me how much I want it? Or did you intentionally not tell me so you could get what you wanted? Shit." She looks at the sky. Her hands are on her hips. "I should not be crying right now."

I reach for her again, but Luca grabs my arm.

My gaze slices to him in fury, but he isn't fazed.

"I thought," Sadie starts, "I thought you …" She shakes her head. "It doesn't matter now."

"It does matter," I rush to say. "Tell me what you're thinking. I want to hear it. I want to know every thought that's passing through your head right now. It matters to me. You matter to me, and I want to be here for you."

"I can't," she whispers. "I don't know what to think right now. It's a lot."

"Yeah, it is, but please don't shut me out. I'm here, Sadie. For all of it. To fight for it. You. Us."

She cries harder, and I know deep in my soul that no matter what I say right now, it's not going to help her. I want to scream *pick me, this me. Pick us.*

But I don't.

Instead, I nod. "What do you want me to do? Whatever you want, it's yours."

She stares at me as if this version of me is unfamiliar, and I hate every second of it.

"I want space. I need time to think about all this." Then she erupts into more tears.

I can't even pretend to know what she's feeling right now.

Fuck.

I want to hold her, hug her, kiss her until her pain goes away.

She starts to walk away, her arms looped with Brooke's, and I finally say what I should have said earlier.

"I didn't tell you that you wanted the space because I was there the day you pitched your reason to Mrs. Whittaker." Hopefully, she will give me one more minute of her time.

She turns to me, and I let out a breath.

Yes.

That's my girl.

"I was also there every time you spoke about Sips and Stories, and Sadie, baby, let me tell you, your passion between the two was as clear as the blue sky. One you were doing for someone else, and one you were doing for you."

More tears fall down her cheeks. I need to wrap this up because I hate being the reason she hurts.

"You wanted to find yourself again, and I thought that if I told you why you wanted this space for the bakery, you'd pick that over Sips and Stories again. That's all I want for you, Sadie. I want you to get everything you want in life, and that means the store of your dreams and not anyone else's."

But Sadie doesn't reply to my confession. Brooke tugs her arm gently, and Sadie follows her into the bakery. The faint click of the door locking is like a punch to the gut.

Like the door to the future I was so convinced I had this morning is gone.

Vanished.

In seconds.

All over again.

CHAPTER TWENTY-NINE

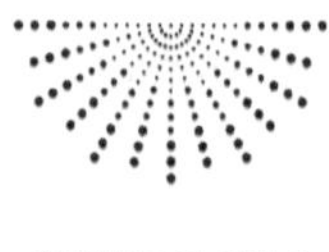

HUDSON

Beer sloshes over my hand.

Again.

"Motherfucking stupid piece of tr—"

"Okay, all right." Two hands land on my shoulder and guide me away from the tap behind the bar. "That's a bit much for the customers, let alone anyone in general, to hear right now," Betty says before stiffly ushering me away from our diners.

I sigh and then shake her off.

"Sorry."

"I know you are, but if you're just going to be a grump and shout incoherent profanity, I think the best place for that is anywhere but here."

"I need to work," I tell her and step for the bar again, but she stops me.

"You need to take time off."

"Betty," I warn.

"Hudson," she warns back. "You. Need. A. Break."

I start to argue, but then I notice the prying eyes. There's a mix of tourists and locals, and it's enough for me to step back and take a breath.

I need a distraction, yes, but I don't need an audience, and that's exactly what we have.

"Yeah. Okay."

"Go for a walk or something. Get some air."

I nod.

"It's all going to work out, Boss. Just give it time."

I huff and walk around her.

She has no idea what she's talking about.

The last time someone told me something similar, I lost everything and ended up right back in the same place as before.

I push on the door a little too hard, and it flies open.

"Oh shit," someone says on the other side.

I want to not give a shit if I hit someone with the door, but no matter how much I hate life right now, I don't want to let myself sink to the level I did before. Sadie might not want anything to do with me, but she would be disappointed if I fell again.

"Sorry, man, I …" My words trail off as I come face to face with Carver Watkins and Archer Hittman.

The three of us stand frozen, staring at one another. While I'm stuck in shock, my former best friends and teammates look relieved.

What are the fucking odds of this right now? I don't need this, this reminder of how far my life has fallen. Yet somehow, that thought isn't enough to make me move my feet and walk away.

"Hey," Carver says first.

"Hi."

"My, uh, my sister is getting married at the lodge this weekend," Archer adds, jerking a thumb over his right shoulder.

They're here because of convenience, not for any other reason.

Sweet.

Then again, I haven't kept in touch with anyone since I left, so how did they know where to find me? They knew I was from here, but I didn't tell anyone I was moving back.

"We called your brother," Carver says quickly. "Luca."

"Three years later," I shout before I can think better of it.

"We tried to call you back when …" Archer's words trail off. "But you changed your number."

It's true—I changed my number after only a couple of weeks.

These were my best friends.

I didn't just lose hockey that day, and that's what hit me the most. If they weren't going to call after a measly two weeks, my mind was made up that they weren't ever going to call. I was going to erase as much of that life as I could.

Now, yes, I see that might have been a rash choice, but it doesn't change the fact they never tried harder to reach me.

"You should have showed up at my door or called the next day or the day after that or—"

"You never called us either," Carver snaps. "You didn't reach out. So we gave you space because we thought that's what you wanted."

His words are like a slap in the face.

Space.

I loathe that word.

"But you clearly didn't want space. We just didn't know that."

"Yeah, man, we were just doing what we thought was best."

The lack of communication on both sides was high back then. I can't blame them for how I handled things, and I can't blame them for not knowing what I wanted if I wasn't telling them.

If the roles were reversed, what would I do? How would I help someone? We all started together, and our careers were just taking off. Life was busy, and our commitment to the team took up a lot of our time. Like Archer just said, they were doing what they thought was best.

Fuck.

The same way I treated Sadie by not telling her about the space between her bakery and my bar.

I didn't intend to hurt her, and they didn't intend to hurt me.

I let out a breath.

"When's the wedding?" I ask.

"Tomorrow."

"Cool, I'll—ugh, I'll send a case of wine over. My treat."

Archer tilts his head. "Is everything okay?"

"Yep."

They both watch me cautiously. When I think they will head into the bar for a drink, Luca rounds the corner and shouts my name.

"Hudson!"

Archer, Carver, and I all glance his way as he walks up.

"No shit, you came. I was just coming to tell him you were in town," Luca says with a grin.

I glance between them.

"They messaged me on the gram since you don't have social media, and I gave them my number."

Awesome.

"This is great timing because Hudson here could use a friend, and I'm in crunch mode trying to land a build with the devil herself."

What the hell is my brother talking about?

"I don't need a friend."

"Last time life didn't work out your way, you shut everyone out. I'm not letting it happen again. Luckily, these two are in town at the perfect moment. Fate is here, boys, don't waste it."

Luca walks off with his phone to his ear, and all I can think, again, is *what the fuck?*

I watch until he disappears and then glance back at Archer and Carver.

They're both grinning.

"So that's Luca," Carver states.

"That's Luca."

"Should we get a beer?" Archer asks and points to the bar.

I take a breath and then let it out, dropping my chin to my chest. What have I got to lose?

———

"Okay, so let me get this right." Carver takes a pull from his second beer and then sits up taller. "You two hated each other, but now you love her."

"That about sums it up."

"Does she love you?"

I shrug. "I'd like to think so, but it's been two days and all I've got is radio silence."

"She won't answer your calls?" Archer asks as Betty brings us another round. His eyes linger on her a moment longer than normal.

I kick his shin under the table.

"Stop ogling my employee."

He holds his hands up. "She held eye contact with me. I can't leave her hanging."

"Sure," I say, and he chuckles, which in turn causes me to do the same because he's not wrong. I've caught her looking too.

I hate to admit this after having so much animosity toward them, but I missed these guys. It's been a whole hour, and even though so much has changed between us, the ease of being around them hasn't.

"I actually haven't tried to call her."

"What?" Carver says a little too loudly.

"Oh my god, have you learned nothing since we last saw you?"

"Yes, I have."

"Okay. Enlighten us."

I glance between them. "Well, I …"

"You need to call her," Archer says quickly. "You didn't call us, and we didn't call you soon enough. Don't make that mistake again."

"I don't think she wants me to call her."

Carver leans forward. "We thought the same thing, and now look. This is the first time in three years we've all had a beer together. Don't be us. Be better."

I nod, letting their words process.

"If you're not going to call her—"

"I'm going to call her," I cut Archer off. "I just don't know what I'm going to say that she hasn't heard yet. And not to mention, I feel like she deserves more than a phone call. She's been through so much that I just want … I just want to ease the stress of everything she has going on right now. If that means I give her the space she asked for even if I don't want to, so be it."

Both of my friends shake their heads.

"What else can I do?" I ask. "Remodel the bar and build the bookstore and hope that when she does want to talk to me again, I can win her over by showing her how badly I want her to get her dream?"

Their faces light up, and Archer snaps his fingers. "That's exactly what you do."

"That's a great start!"

I study them for a moment as I process everything I'll need to get started and get this in motion. Of course, it'll take months to go from start to finish. I sure as hell don't intend to wait that long to talk to Sadie again, but until she's ready to see me, I'm going to do everything I can to prove that I've meant every single word I've said to her since the moment she knocked on my door.

Me and her, there is no going back.

"Remodeling the space is great, but I have a better idea."

One that hopefully lets me win the girl back sooner rather than later.

"How long are you here?"

"Four days." Carver grins.

"When do we get started?" Archer asks.

"Right now," I stand quickly, my chair screeching as it moves back. The three of us head for the door and for the first time in days, I have a smile on my lips.

I've got my friends back for the weekend, which means there is one more group I need to message right now.

I reach into my pocket and send a quick group text to Linc, my dad, and my brothers. One that is short, sweet, and to the point. A text I should have sent three years ago.

HUDSON

I need your help.

CHAPTER THIRTY

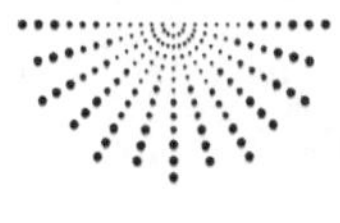

SADIE

I'm losing my mind.

I can almost laugh at that saying because I actually did lose mine.

But now it's back, and it's a lot to pack in.

I roll to my side and pull my comforter all the way to my chin. This has pretty much been my spot for the last three days. The only times I've left were to find food. My dad has checked on me a few times a day, but my answer is always the same when he asks me how I'm doing.

Fine.

Just one word.

At this point, I'm sure he thinks I'm crazy. I'm more distraught over my memory coming back than I was over losing it. Yes, not remembering my mother's funeral sucked, but Hudson made it special for me. He didn't force me to just move past it—he let me go on as if my life just picked up where I left off three years ago.

That means something to me, and I'm not sure how to cope with all of it.

Silent tears start to fall, the way they have at random moments since it all came back to me. I can remember us in Mrs. Whittaker's space and arguing just as clearly as I can remember waking up in Hudson's arms a few days ago to find him watching me. I can remember the way he kissed me good morning and held me and the way he rolled me to my back and showed me how much he cares about me.

I swipe the tears away the best I can.

The emotions I have for him are so overwhelming that I don't know where to start processing first. And the worst part is, I want to call him and get his help. He's the one I want to run to right now, but … I don't know what to do.

I inhale and then sit up.

I cannot keep crying over this.

A knock sounds at my door, and like clockwork, my dad pokes his head in.

"Hey, hun, how are you?"

"Fi—" I start to say but stop myself. "Why did you let me keep working at the bakery?"

My question catches him off guard, but he nods and sits on the corner of my bed. This topic is long overdue, but now is as good a time as any.

"You said you wanted it, and for a time, I think you did. But no matter how many times I could see that it wasn't what you wanted anymore, you held your head high and said that it was."

"Oh."

"You know," he goes on, "if you still want to sell it to Brooke, even knowing everything you know now, I think you should."

My next breath hitches, and the tears start again. "But I made it this far just fine. I can't just sell it and erase Mom's biggest memory. The thing she loved most."

Dad grins and shakes his head. "What she loved most was

you and your brother, and if you want me to be brutally honest, she'd have my hide if she knew I let you keep that place this long knowing it wasn't your dream."

I huff.

"Yeah, well, Hudson took that dream and then he took my next one too."

"I see," Dad says and looks out the window. His lips twist as he prepares to say more.

"Just spit it out, Dad."

"I don't believe that Hudson took your dream. He took the space, which if we want to get technical, you didn't file the paperwork on time the first go-around anyway and the building sold to him. That's life, sweetheart, not Hudson."

"Okay, then explain why he never told me about the two of us wanting Mrs. Whittaker's place, huh? He intentionally didn't tell me about it."

"Did you ask him why?"

"I did."

"And what was his answer?"

"That the way I talked about Sips and Stories versus how I talked about the bakery were not the same, and he didn't want me to question my dreams again. He didn't want me to miss out on getting what I wanted in life."

The old Hudson would have never said that and meant it. The new Hudson would, but I just don't know how to forget the old one. I've known that one the longest.

"So what's the problem? It sounds an awful lot like why I didn't tell you that you wanted it or why Linc never mentioned it, either."

"You both knew?" I snap.

"We did, yes, so did Brooke, but buying a new business was the last thing you needed to worry about. You'd made it very clear you wanted to do this your own way, and we did our best to respect that. You can't be mad at anyone over this one."

"But I can, Dad. Especially with Hudson."

"Why?"

"Because it's different with him. We were … more, and he didn't think I was strong enough to make that choice on my own. That sounds a lot like the old Hudson." I blow out a breath. "The new Hudson would have trusted me and told me to go after what I want."

"And what do you want?"

"To own my own business that I build, to live on my own and create my own home, to go after a life that no one chose but me."

The outburst takes me by surprise. The old me would have never responded like that. The old me would have just accepted what life had given her and maintained it.

Old.

New.

Old.

New.

What is wrong with me? I sound like I'm broken.

Like before, though, Dad is unfazed as he nods. "This is a good plan. I want to help."

"Oh, Dad, you do not. You just don't want to see me cry anymore."

"You can stay here till the end of the month, but then you're out."

"What?"

"Sweetheart, I'm an old man, and my thirty-year-old daughter still lives with me. I'm ready to be on my own again."

"You're kicking me out?"

"No. I'm making sure you pick yourself for once. That you pick what you want and not what others think you should pick."

"Oh." Great, he spit my own words back at me.

"I know you don't want to hear this, but I sense that's what Hudson was trying to do in his own way."

I groan.

"You need to talk to him."

"I know, but it's weird. I'm not sure which version of me wants to talk to him. Part of me wants to yell at him for how he handled things, and the other … well, he's the one I want to vent to about all this."

Dad nods slowly.

"Stop nodding," I scold with a laugh. "You're supposed to advise me, not just agree with everything that comes out of my mouth."

"You know which side you really want. So my advice would be meaningless."

"But what if I pick the wrong one?"

"You won't because you already know what you want."

"But what if—"

"Sadie," he pushes off the bed to stand, "you've got this, but it isn't going to happen by sitting in this room."

I don't know what will happen next, but I do know that even though I keep saying there is an old Hudson and new Hudson, the fact is, the old Hudson is just that—old. I can sit here telling myself I don't believe that, but I do.

The other thing I know? I miss the heck out of Hudson Asher, and the two of us need to talk. He may have confessed that he didn't want me to forget my dream. Fine. I get it. But he still bought the space out from under me. I'm not okay with that. There has to be something I'm missing.

I'm just not so sure I'm ready for the answer.

———

By lunch, I'm stepping into the bakery's kitchen, headed for the office.

"Sadie!" Brooke beams as she spots me. "What are you doing here?"

I don't answer right away. Instead, I wrap my arms around my best friend.

She hugs me back, tight.

I finally step back. "I still want to sell this place to you."

"You do?" Her lips twist as if she's unsure what else to ask me.

I nod. "My dad reminded me this morning that Mom wouldn't want me to stay here if I didn't love it. She'd want me to sell it to someone who would put their heart and soul into it, and that person is still you."

She sticks her bottom lip out and then fans her face.

"I'm going to make you both proud."

"I know you will, but until we make this official, I have some things to do with the books."

I grab the laptop from the office, plate up a pastry, make an iced coffee, and then sit where Bartley, Marty, and Phil normally sit.

There are still booths on Main Street from our last street festival. Between working here for the afternoon and working myself up to go to Hudson, people-watching will be a great distraction.

I turn my computer on and get about fifteen minutes of work done before I see Luca pull up in his truck. He hops out, a man I don't recognize with him. He's huge though—broad shoulders, maybe six feet tall, and shaggy hair.

He looks familiar.

They both go straight for the door to Mrs. Whittaker's space-— or well, now Hudson's, and my curiosity turns to anger in a flash.

Buying that place while knowing I wanted it was cruel. Like Hudson never changed. I feel so stupid and yet, ugh, I want to know why. Why would he go through everything in the last month with me just to screw me over, again?

I don't get much time to think it over before Miles steps into the bakery.

He looks around and as soon as he spots me, his lips split into a grin.

"Just the woman I was looking for." He struts toward me.

He sets a folded piece of paper on the table, taps it, and then shoves his hands in his pockets.

"What's that?"

"It's for you."

"Obviously." I grin.

I don't move to grab it, and he says, "Read it so I can leave."

He glances at Brooke, who quickly looks away as if she weren't watching us.

I open the note. All it says is Marriage of Convenience Margarita.

I read it again and then flip it over as if there's more information on the backside.

"I don't get it."

"Me either, but if you want answers, Hudson is next door."

At that, he turns and walks out.

CHAPTER THIRTY-ONE

HUDSON

"What did she say?"

Miles shrugs as he walks into the space.

"I don't know. I left after she read it, like you said."

"You didn't wait for her reaction?"

"She asked what it was, and I said to come over here for answers and then left."

Okay. He's not wrong. I did tell him to make it short and sweet, so she had to come find me.

I glance around the room where Luca, Carter, Archer, and Linc are all building shelves. I'm not making anything permanent. She was very clear that she wanted to do this on her own, but when she arrives, I want her to see her vision coming to life. I want her to see that I was listening, that I'm still the same guy I have been this past month.

I want her to see how much I love her.

With my friends and family hard at work, I walk to the front window and peek out.

There's no sign of her leaving the bakery.

CHAPTER THIRTY-TWO

SADIE

"I'm going to the bank in the morning to go over finances, and when I get back, we can go over—"

My brother walks in.

"Afternoon, ladies," he greets us and then hugs me. I'm standing by the register with Brooke. "I think I'll take a half dozen lemon bars, please."

He grins, but it's different from normal.

I cross my arms and lean my hip to the counter. "I made you a batch two days ago. Did you already eat them all?"

He makes a yikes face and hands Brooke his debit card.

I glare a little harder, but he has no reaction to it, and he doesn't say a word.

"Later," he finally says and heads for the door. "Oh,"—he snaps his fingers—"I almost forgot this." He walks back to me and hands me a note, just like the one Miles brought me about twenty minutes ago. This one reads Brother's Best Friend Brandy.

"Seriously, what is this?" I snap.

Linc just tosses his arms up and shrugs.

"I'm not the one you need to ask."

"I'm not—"

He's gone before I can finish.

I march to the door and watch my brother duck into the space next door.

What the hell are they doing over there?

I'll admit that I'm curious, but not enough to face Hudson.

Not yet.

CHAPTER THIRTY-THREE

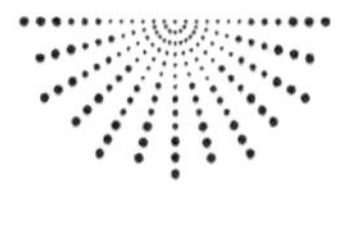

HUDSON

"Well?"

"I'm not so sure she wants to talk to you," Linc says and then sets the box of lemon bars on the counter. All the guys take a break to grab one.

"Are these the same bars you said were subpar?" Archer asks.

"Same recipe," I admit. "But I think Brooke was the one baking this morning."

Carver tsks and shakes his head at me. "I wouldn't want to come talk to you either."

I sigh and look at the door.

She's going to come, right?

CHAPTER THIRTY-FOUR

SADIE

I spot Luca just before he steps into the bakery.

He smiles and joins me at my table.

"You can skip the small talk," I tell him.

He smirks, and I swear his cheeks turn a light shade of pink.

"I'm just trying to help him, Sadie."

He hands me the note.

"Three years ago, he wouldn't have asked me for help, but he did this time. We both know he changed for the better the moment you showed up at his door."

I clear my throat and open the note.

Age Gap Mai Tai.

For some reason, this one makes me smile.

"He's next door, if no one has mentioned that yet."

"They have."

Luca stands.

"So, are you going to come?"

I shake my head. "See you later, Luca."

His shoulders drop, and he leaves.

"What's going on?" Brooke asks.

"He's matching romance tropes with drinks and naming them."

"Who?"

"Hudson."

She takes the notes from the corner of the table and looks through them.

"But why?"

"Because I told him I thought the idea would be fun for how I shelved the books at Sips and Stories."

"Oh, well, that's kind of cute," Brooke says with a swoon-worthy smile, but she cuts it short when she sees me glaring at her. "What?"

"Why is he reminding me of this all while knowing the place he just bought would have been the perfect spot?"

She shrugs. "You should go ask him."

I nod slowly.

Yeah, I know I should.

I'm just not ready for which version of Hudson I'm going to get.

CHAPTER THIRTY-FIVE

HUDSON

"Why isn't she coming over?"

I switch my gaze from the front window to the guys behind me. They all look away quickly.

I suppose I wasn't really looking for an answer. I know the reason, but I was convinced that by reminding her of something she shared with me while we were together, she'd come to talk to me. Let me explain. All of it this time.

"Archer," I call his name and then hand him the last note. I could go all day with these, but the bakery closes soon, and honestly, if she doesn't come over after four notes, I don't think she's going to after five or six.

Archer grabs the note from me and walks out the door without a word.

Linc walks in from the back with some flowers and the books Sadie left at my apartment. The blueprints of ideas are on the counter. I have books, flowers, and shelves for the tropes with drink names. The only thing missing is the big windows, but I can't give her that until she comes over here and picks out a blueprint.

Fuck.

What am I going to do if she doesn't come over after this one?

How am I going to convince her to give me another chance?

CHAPTER THIRTY-SIX

SADIE

The man who got out of Luca's truck is next.

"Hi," he says as he eyes Brooke behind the counter.

She smiles, shakes her head, and points to me.

He walks over and holds out the note for me to take.

I grab it, but he doesn't let go. Instead, he looks me in the eye and says, "Don't give up on him. I did once, and I promised myself that I'd never do it again. He's a good man, Sadie. Give him a chance to prove it."

At that, he lets go and walks out.

My bottom lip starts to shake as tears prick my eyes.

Promise me that when your memory comes back, this is the version of me you'll remember.

That moment with Hudson comes back to me in a rush.

I close my eyes in an attempt to not cry, but as soon as I do, a vision of his face the other day hits me.

The way he *knew* I remembered everything.

The way he pleaded with me not to walk away.

He told me that was his biggest fear for us, and I made his fear a reality without a second thought.

Looks like we both have things we need to say to each other.

I open the note and smile.

Old-Fashioned Enemies-to-Lovers.

I take a breath and stand.

It's now or never.

Maybe I'll step through that door, and the old Hudson will appear, but perhaps I'll walk through it, and everything will feel right again.

There's only one way to find out.

"Brooke, I'm going to—"

The door to the bakery swings open and a flustered Hudson fills the doorway. The sapphire eyes I've grown to love settle on me.

"What are you doing?" he asks as if he's breathless.

I open my mouth to answer, but he beats me to it.

"I'm sending you notes and hinting that you need to come next door. Clearly, there's a reason. Why are you still here?"

I cross my arms. He's not the one who gets to be mad.

"Excuse me for—"

"Ah," he cuts me off and jerks his thumb over his shoulder. "Over there."

And then he walks out.

My jaw drops.

The nerve!

I let out a huff as I march from the bakery to the space next door.

No way in hell am I letting him act like that after everything he's done.

I jerk the door open and blaze in. "Don't you ever talk to me like—"

I stop short, a gasp stealing my next breath.

Hudson is standing in the middle of the room, next to the counter where Mrs. Whittaker used to have her handmade jewelry. There are flowers covering it, along with more in each corner of the space. Six bookshelves round the back of the room; each one has one book with a notecard displayed next to it. I'm too far away to see what's written on them, but from the notes sitting on the table next door, I have a pretty good hunch as to what they say.

There's a table and a couple of chairs in front of one of the shelves, and it's clear that he took them from the bar. The table has three rolls on it, and they look exactly like what Luca was holding earlier today when he got out of his truck.

"What is this?" I ask.

Hudson takes a breath, shoving his hands into his jeans. "It's Sips and Stories."

"How?" I say quickly before I start to cry, again. "I don't own this, and I'm not leasing it from you. That's not how I want to do this."

"I know, but I was hoping we could do it together."

"Together?"

He grabs something off the counter that I didn't see with all the flowers in front of it.

It's a legal-size document.

He steps toward me and hands it over.

I read through it quickly.

My name is listed right next to his under the purchasers' names, and it's dated for the day my memory came back. The only thing missing is my signature.

"When I showed up that day, I was bringing this to you. I wanted it to be a surprise."

Oh, I think we were all surprised.

"You … you bought this for us?"

"For you," he corrects me, taking another step forward. "I'm just hoping you want to share it with me."

"You want to share the bookstore?" I ask to clarify.

He shakes his head.

"I want to share your dreams, your life, *our* life. Everything."

He moves to grab the blue rolls off the other table and hands them to me.

"I asked Luca to give you a few options on how you could remodel this place. With me or without me, I want you to have everything you want—but for the record, I really hope you choose to do it with me."

My heart starts to race.

It's him. The Hudson I fell in love with.

My hands start to shake. I still have a chance to keep my promise to him. I plan to, but in order for us to move forward, we can't have any more secrets.

"Were you going to tell me about Mrs. Whittaker's deal with us?"

"I don't know." He inhales a breath. "I wanted to, and in my head, I knew that was the right move, but I can't tell you for sure that I would have followed through. I meant it when I said the only reason I didn't tell you is because your dream of having your own place was so strong, I was worried that if I told you everything, you'd feel obligated to do something else instead."

"You should have trusted me."

"I do trust you," he says quickly.

"Then you should have told me everything."

"I was scared, okay?" He runs a hand through his hair and spins. His hand rests on his hips for a moment before he turns around. "I'd just fallen in love with the most incredible woman to ever walk this earth, and I was terrified as hell that if I told you everything, you'd remember a version of me who didn't exist anymore, and you'd leave. Turns out, no matter which choice I made, I lost you."

I place the blueprints on the counter and cross my arms.

"Oh, so you get to decide how this ends now?"

His gaze darts to meet mine.

He's still studying me as I say, "Because the way I see it is, I own half this place, and that means you're stuck with me."

"I …"

"Oh, you have nothing to say now?"

I take another step toward him, closing the distance between us, and a small smile tugs at his lips.

"As co-owner," I continue, "I have some rules, and I suggest not speaking until I'm done listing them."

He nods.

"First, you will never, *ever* keep something from me. No matter how scared or nervous or whatever you are, you come to me. You *always* come to me."

He nods again.

"Second, I call dibs on the apartment above this place because my father told me I needed to move out by the end of the month."

Hudson presses his lips together as he tries not to laugh.

"Third, the blueprint we use will be one we pick together. You like the windows in the bar. I like the windows in the bar. We will decide together."

"Well, that's why—"

"I'm not done yet," I cut him off, and he nods.

"And the fourth rule, the *most important* rule is"—I move to stand right in front of him, reach up and stroke his cheek, and the breath he lets out relaxes his entire body—"that I love you too."

Hudson cups my cheeks like I'm his and slams his mouth to mine. He kisses me as if we have time to make up for, and he's right.

I wrap my arms around his neck as he lifts me to wrap my legs around him. He starts moving toward the back of the room.

"Where are we going?" I ask. As excited as I am about what's on his mind, I'm equally excited to see those blueprints.

I've never been this close to my dream, and I have Hudson to thank for that.

"Upstairs, to what you think will be your apartment."

I laugh. "To what I think?"

He sets me down at the back door.

"Yeah, you haven't seen them yet, but none of those designs include two living spaces."

"What? Why? What will you do with this one?"

"You mean, what will we do?"

I nod.

"We will knock out the wall that separates them and make one big apartment where we will live together."

"Oh, is that so?"

"Yes."

"Promise me," I say, repeating the words he once said to me. "Promise me that no matter what life puts in our path, it will be you and me together."

He smirks right before he kisses me.

"I promise."

EPILOGUE

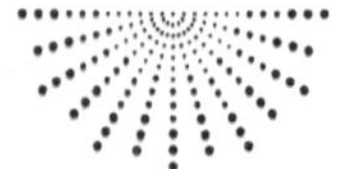

HUDSON - ONE YEAR LATER

Luca made space in his schedule to do the remodel in the winter. Now, we are coming up to the one-year anniversary of when Sadie showed up at my doorstep and demanded I let her move in with me, and our store has officially been open for two months.

It's been a wild two months, and I don't see it letting up anytime soon.

I spit out my mouthwash and turn off all the lights before I head down to the bar.

Even though the bar and Sips and Stories are now one big open space, they each have their own main entrance. Sadie and I went back and forth over whether we should give the entire place a new name, but in the end, we decided that Hudson's and Sips and Stories both deserved their own names. Both represent a piece of what we fought to get back, so it didn't feel right to take that from either one of us.

I pass through the kitchen, stopping outside the office to talk to Ian.

"Hey, is everything ready for tonight?" I ask.

"Yes, sir."

"And she has no idea."

"None."

I knock on the doorframe and smile.

"Good."

Then I make my way out to the main room. Turns out, moving the bar top would have added time to the remodel, so the bar top is still in the same place. But now, instead of it being surrounded by high-top tables, there is a mix of tall tables, standard tables, couches, and comfy chairs. The entire place looks more homey. Just the way Sadie and I wanted it. The side that holds the bookstore, Mrs. Whittaker's old space, has more couches, but the space is so open that customers can purchase their books and enjoy a drink, too.

Sadie is behind the counter of Sips, laughing with a customer who has a stack of books between them.

Most of the bookstore holds romance books, and from what Sadie told me, I knew that it was a big market, but damn, I did not expect the bookstore to be neck and neck with the bar on profits each month.

The door to the bookstore opens and Brooke walks in with a pink box of baked goods. Sadie sells them in the store, but she switches it up each day to whatever Brooke feels like baking.

I hear my brothers laughing behind me, and as I glance around, I feel like a sappy sap thinking of how this is actually my life right now. Add in the fact that The Rockets have asked me to officially be their assistant coach and life is amazing.

"This place is packed," Luca says.

"Again," Miles adds.

"Oh, look there's Simon Stone," my dad says and waves to Betty Banks walking in with her grandson, Tobias Banks, and Simon. Both Tobias and Simon write romance books.

That's why the crowd is so big today.

"Is it just the two of them signing today?" Miles asks. His

tone loses a fraction of its cheeriness when Tobias's sister, Quinn, walks in behind the group. "I'm out," he says before I can answer his signing question.

He stops to shake Tobias's hand and then Simon's, then he leans in to hug Betty. Quinn smiles at him, but he just walks right by her like he didn't even see her.

I shake my head. Miles can be stubborn and strong headed, but I've never seen anyone get him as worked up as Quinn Banks. She only comes here a few weeks every summer and then over Christmas, so I have no clue when the two of them could have created this feud he thinks they have.

"Oh fuck, who invited Shay?" Luca whisper-snaps at me.

"Well, this is a local business, and she is a local, soooo …"

He groans and walks off to get a drink at the bar, then finds a spot out of her view.

I chuckle to myself.

I see my brothers every Sunday at breakfast, and they tell me everything from the nails Luca bought on sale last week to the new car remodel Miles is working on, but I get the feeling they're keeping some details to themselves.

A hand rubs up my back and over my shoulder.

"Why did Miles leave?" Sadie asks as she steps in front of me and presses a quick kiss to my lips.

"I'm not really sure. Remind me to ask him at breakfast this weekend."

"You got it. Hey, did you get those bags we sorted for the giveaway winners?"

I nod toward the back office. "Yep, they're in the back. I'll go get them."

She laces her hand with mine. "I'll come with you."

I step through the doorway and head for the corner where I put the bag, but I hear the door click behind me.

I spin to see a naughty grin on Sadie's lips.

"What are you doing?" I ask, standing up straighter and forgetting about the bag. I'm more interested in whatever she's up to.

"I just thought that with a busy schedule ahead of us, we could have a minute alone."

I nod. "And what should we do with this time?"

She saunters toward me and sits on the desk, pulling me toward her with the belt buckle.

"I think we can come up with something."

I'm leaning in to kiss her when there's a knock at the door.

"Sadie, Hudson," Linc's voice comes through the door. "Someone wants to talk to the owner out front."

Sadie beams. "That's me."

I chuckle at how quickly she can put on her business face but swell with pride as I watch her walk out the door.

She's got everything she wanted in life.

I reach my hand into my pocket and twirl the diamond ring around my pinky.

If I'm lucky, by the end of the night, I will too.

Want more from Hudson and Sadie?
Get an exclusive bonus scene of them in the future here.

Ready to find out which Asher sibling gets book two?
Find out when you pre-order Loving You today!

BONUS EPILOGUE

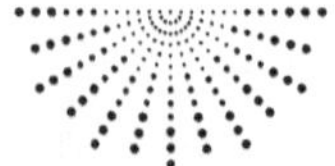

SADIE – FIVE YEARS LATER

This place is still just as cold as it was five years ago.

The sound of skates racing across the ice and a crowd cheering on the players fill the bleachers around me.

The Rockets are up by one, but their opponents aren't ready to give up just yet. There are two minutes left. I spot Hudson across the ice; his arms are crossed as his gaze remains laser focused on his team.

It's Hudson's first year as head coach for the Wind Valley team—Beacher retired—and he's dominating it. The Rockets are undefeated, and even though I can see the stress line forming between my husband's brows all the way from over here, I have no doubts that his team is going to win tonight, too.

Suddenly, the crowd erupts as one of Hudson's boys has taken control of the puck and is racing to the other net.

He pulls his stick back so quickly that I almost miss it.

Then the buzzer sounds, and it's full-on chaos.

I wrap my hand around the baby girl strapped to my chest, bundled in just enough layers to keep warm. I pull back the top of her little purple bear fleece suit and kiss her little bald head.

"Daddy just won," I whisper.

She's sound asleep even with the crowd celebrating behind us.

Everyone begins to file out to the main room, where there is heat, and I'm right there with them.

While families chat and greet their kids as they leave the locker room, I stay near the trophy wall, bouncing side to side softly.

"That was a wild game," Luca says, joining me and squatting to see if Maddy is awake.

"If she's awake, I get to hold her first," Miles says quickly.

"Nope. As her grandpa, I call dibs," their dad chimes in right behind them.

As if the chaos of the town's team winning isn't enough, Carver and Archer showed up for today's game, and as soon as they make their appearance in the lobby of the rink, everything grows louder.

The two smile over the crowd in greeting, and then they give their full attention to their fans.

We'll have plenty of time to catch up back in Lovers since they're staying with Hudson and me over the weekend.

The main room thins a little over the next half hour as people go home for the night. A few stop to tell me how amazing Hudson has been for the boys.

The feeling has been mutual over the years.

Hudson is the last to leave the locker room, like most game nights.

He walks through the crowd, shaking hands with parents and high-fiving his players, but his sights are set on me. Even after all these years, my heart beats a little faster when he smiles just for me.

"There are my girls," he says quietly, pressing his lips to

mine. I peel back Maddy's hood, and he kisses the top of her head.

"Did she wake up during the game?"

"Just once, so I dipped out to feed her, and then she was right back to sleep."

"We got lucky with this little sleeper," he says and then hugs his dad and brothers.

Since the summer I hit my head, life has been a whirlwind of events. Moving in with Hudson, opening Sips and Stories, getting engaged, running two business with Hudson, watching him fall back in love with the ice, getting married, and now parenting.

We've been parents for six months as of today.

Maybe that's why my heart is racing. This whirlwind isn't over yet.

As soon as Hudson is done for the night, and we're back on the road for Lovers, I get to tell him that we get to do it again.

Our life together is great, but it's about to get so much better.

MORE BOOKS BY JAMI ROGERS

For the full list of books and series by Jami Rogers, please visit Jami's website by clicking here.

or

Scan the QR code below.

FOLLOW JAMI

Want more from Jami?

Join Jami's mailing list for exclusive bonus epilogues, giveaways, and all the book news!

Visit her website
www.authorjamirogers.com

Or join her Facebook group
Jami Rogers Readers

facebook.com/AuthorJamiRogers

instagram.com/authorjamirogers

bookbub.com/authors/authorjamirogers

goodreads.com/jamirogers

tiktok.com/@authorjamirogers

ACKNOWLEDGMENTS

Thank you, Hang Le, Julie, Dana, and Jenny, for helping me publish this fantastic book. I'm obsessed.

Cheers to the next book!

ABOUT THE AUTHOR

My name is Jami Rogers, and I write small-town, steamy romance. My favorite tropes to write (and read) are enemies to lovers, friends to lovers, roommates, and my best friend's brother/sister.

I like to read, write, watch movies/TV, and spend time with my family. I'm horrible at returning phone calls and prefer to text, but still struggle to hit the little blue arrow to send a message once I'm finished typing my reply. My husband does 90% of the cooking in our house. Not because I'm busy – I'm just simply a bad cook.

facebook.com/AuthorJamiRogers

instagram.com/authorjamirogers

goodreads.com/jamirogers

bookbub.com/profile/jami-rogers

tiktok.com/@authorjamirogers

www.ingramcontent.com/pod-product-compliance
Lightning Source LLC
Chambersburg PA
CBHW021413010826
48972CB00014B/2063